Secrets of San Blas

Charles Farley

Pineapple Press, Inc.
Sarasota, Florida

Inquiries should be addressed to:

Pineapple Press, Inc.
P.O. Box 3889
Sarasota, Florida 34230

www.pineapplepress.com

Library of Congress Cataloging in Publication Data

Farley, Charles,
Secrets of San Blas / Charles Farley. -- 1st ed.
    p. cm.
ISBN 978-1-56164-514-5 (alk. paper)
1. Physicians--Florida--Fiction. 2. Lighthouses--Fiction. 3.
Murder--Investigation--Fiction. 4. Port Saint Joe (Fla.)--Fiction. I.
Title.
PS3606.A695S43 2012
813'.6--dc23
                                2011043499

First Edition
10 9 8 7 6 5 4 3 2 1

Design by Shé Hicks
Printed and bound in the USA

Author's Note

Parts of the following story are based on events surrounding an actual murder that occurred in the spring of 1938 at the Cape San Blas Lighthouse near Port St. Joe, Florida. All the rest is made up.

What is man? A miserable little pile of secrets.
Andre Malraux

The light. It was the incessant light. Every twenty seconds. He counted them off: one-mississippi, two-mississippi, three-mississippi . . . twenty-mississippi. And the white beam flashed across the sea. Again. Each as clear and quick as the slash of a knife.

It was almost dawn. Almost time. He could see a pink hint of light creeping up just beyond St. Vincent Island. Soon the low-lying clouds would flush to red—the color of blood. He could already smell its metallic odor. See its crimson rush. Hear the gurgle of his final breath.

Sailors take warning.

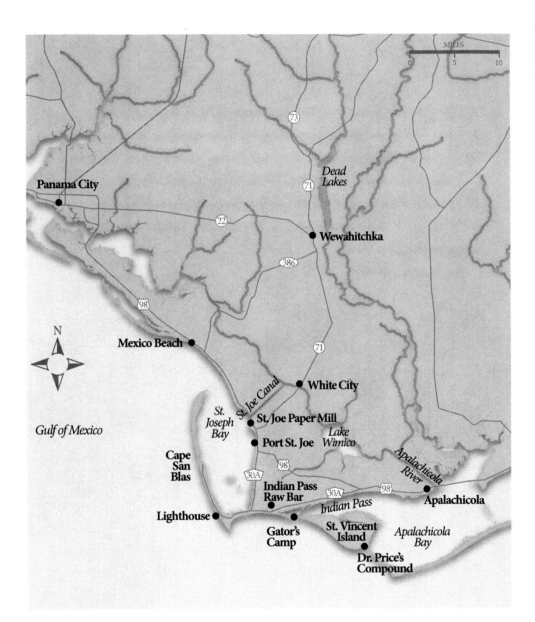

Chapter One

The doctor was dying. This morning, he awoke, as usual, in pain. The malaise was so acute that he was nauseated. He wanted to just lie there in bed, but he knew it would do no good. Once awake, his suffering would only continue. It was a saturating sense of physical, emotional, and spiritual weariness—part old age, part arthritic aches that he had inherited from his mother—and, more than anything else, just the repetitive routine of his life and the everyday dreariness of the existence in which he found himself mired.

His days were numbered, like those of a death-row inmate, only he didn't know exactly what his number would be. But he did know, as surely as he did when he made a fatal diagnosis, that he was a goner. Just a matter of time. And it angered him, made him despondent and testy most of the time. But he didn't know what to do about it, because there was no specific ailment that the doctor could actually treat. In other words, he couldn't heal himself, as the biblical proverb advised. He just felt this gnawing, deep down inside of himself, as familiar now as his own breathing, which he was convinced by now would only too soon cease.

As accustomed as he was to death, as his profession demanded, you would think he would have come to terms with it by now. But he had not. He abhorred and feared the thought of it, of disintegrating, just like that, like a firecracker on the Fourth of July, gone and forgotten in one fiery, trifling pop. Not that he expected to go that suddenly and swiftly, although at times he wished he would, particularly when the aches and pains so disheartened him. In those moments, he often devised the detailed means of putting an end to it all in one fell, painless swoop. Pills, drugs in various combinations, all readily available to him. Spectacular crashes off rural bridges into muddy rivers or abysmal bays where he and his old Ford would sink silently into that deep, dark night now and forever.

He hadn't quite worked it all out yet, but he was certain he would as the time grew nearer. It would be something that would surprise and cheer his few friends, make them laugh out loud and leave them a funny, final retort to the long, rambling conversation that was his life. As he drove around the sleepy north Florida town of Port St. Joe, making his rounds, conducting house calls, avoiding the confounded telephone, he knew it would come to him, gradually and naturally, the final solution that would make some sense to him, not of his life, but, at least, its impending end.

As for his remaining days, the doctor was content to do the best he could to keep their little village by the sea as healthy as he could, no matter how disgruntled he was becoming and how senseless the disasters—both major and minute—now seemed to him. He would just keep mending the mutilated, somehow salving their wounds, internal as well as external, and holding on, unassumingly from one doleful day to the next.

There was only one antidote that made it all bearable. Dr. Van Berber slowly reached for the dark brown bottle of morphine that rested in its usual place on his bedside table. He had learned by trial and error over the years, since his first wife Annie's disappearance now more than a decade ago, how to measure the narcotic's thrice daily portions in just the right amounts to ease his pain and permit him to function with minimal drowsiness and constipation as Port St. Joe's only general practitioner. He measured the dose and mixed it with a waiting glass of water, now disgustingly warm. He watched the swirling little cloud of brown solace dissolve into a murky, muddy pool and then sipped its bitterness while sitting up in a pile of pillows on his old, familiar bed.

As the drug slowly entered his system, he lay still with his eyes closed and listened to the overture of the new day: bluebirds and mockingbirds singing in the crape myrtle below his window, sea gulls arguing on the beach down the street, a woodpecker tapping on the rotting oak in his backyard, car wheels scrunching down the crumbled shell road that passed his house, Jewel in the kitchen downstairs preparing breakfast. Jewel Jackson, sweet Jewel, his maid and cook since shortly after his third wife, Jennie, had divorced him nearly three years before, was now his single constant. Bless her. Without her, he was sure he would remain in bed all day every day. Fortunately, she arrived each weekday morning at around eight o'clock, after dropping her seven year-old son, Marcus, off at school, and by 8:30 she had the doctor's breakfast ready when he had finished showering and dressing.

There had been still another wife between Annie and Jennie, devoted Carrie Jo, his faithful Yankee nurse, whom he had married in 1929, two years after Annie's disappearance. She had been patient with his lingering heartbreak and sorrow about losing Annie. Until she died of lung cancer in 1933, she had been a caring nurse and nurtured him during those first awful, empty days, weeks, months, and then years since Annie, his first true love, had vanished from his life, just like that.

The memories disgorged again, like the bile from a poisoned stomach, as he tried to rise and get out of bed. How he had seen Annie off, for the last time as it would turn out, at the train station in Tallahassee. She had waved goodbye with that funny little tilt of her wrist, as if swatting at a fly, in her bright, white spring dress, auburn hair pulled back off her wide-eyed face, smiling faintly, as he absent-mindedly checked his pocket watch and returned her wave. It would be the last time he was to see her. Somewhere between Tallahassee and Washington, D.C., where she was going to visit her sister, Alexandria, Annie had vanished. Trying to find her had turned out to be a jurisdictional nightmare. No one wanted or cared to take responsibility, since no one was sure exactly where she had disappeared. The conductor remembered last seeing her somewhere near Charleston, South Carolina, returning something to her bag in the overhead rack above her seat. And then came a panicked long-distance telephone call from Alexandria late the following night. Annie had not arrived in Washington on the appointed train at the appointed time. "Where is she?" Alexandria had cried helplessly. "I can't find her." No one else could either. The sheriff in Charleston said he would search, but he never found anything. The federal marshal in charge of interstate railroad security questioned the conductor and other rail personnel. All they knew was that, somewhere around Charleston, Annie and her two bags had left the train never to be seen or heard from again, like a bolt of lightning that's there one second and gone the next, ripping a gaping hole in the doctor's heart.

Lying there in bed, he thought now again for the thousandth time that if he had been more rational, more level-headed in the first few critical hours after Alexandria's call, maybe he could have done something more to find her. But instead Alexandria's panic over the telephone had infectiously overcome him, as if electronically transmitted through the wires, and left him scurrying willy-nilly from train station to train station, official to official, in an aimless, frenetic, futile search. Sometimes, when he had mixed too much whiskey with his nightly dose of morphine, he dreamed vividly that she returned, smiling, bags in hand, to his front door, as if nothing had happened.

Now, eleven years later, he still missed her. Theirs was not a perfect marriage by any means, but neither of them could stay angry for long, and it was never more than a few hours before they needed to confide in each other about some detail or another of everyday life that called out for discussion. More than anything, he missed these private chats with her. Over the years, they had developed their own shorthand language, their own shared, goofy jokes, and their own mutual, screwy way of seeing the world. And all that was gone now.

When the doctor finally entered the kitchen, Jewel, dressed immaculately in a starched white dress, greeted him as usual in her overly saccharine way, mildly annoying the doctor at the start of what he was confident would be another bleak day.

"Sleep well, doctor?" she inquired, as she placed a plate of bacon, eggs, and grits, as well as a big bowl of strawberries and cream, on the kitchen table in front of him.

"Well enough, I guess," the doctor grumbled. "You?"

"Like a log," she chirped, pouring them both a cup of black coffee.

"Hmm, good strawberries. Where're they from?"

"On the back porch this mornin'," Jewel answered, as she dried her hands on the hem of her apron. "Note says they're from May Wingate. They're nice and fresh and sweet, ain't they?"

"Yes and I'm gonna drool red strawberry juice all down the front of me if I'm not careful. I set her son Wayne's broken arm last week and she couldn't pay, so I was hoping for something. Not bad, not bad atall. What else is going on this morning?"

"Oh, not much, Doc. Big news is the openin' of that new paper mill up where Blossom Row used to be, I guess. Got everybody 'round here in a tizzy 'bout that."

"You?"

"No, not really. Looks like the only jobs for colored folks out there are mostly for janitors and porters—low-paying shit jobs that white people don't want, as usual. Pardon my French."

The next day's opening of the St. Joe Paper Company, on March 17, 1938, held about as much interest for the doctor as it did for his maid, despite the fact that he knew it would put a lot people who needed jobs to work, while, at the same time, further decimating the area's forests, spewing smoke from its chimneys, and dumping who knows what kinds of nasty waste and toxic chemicals into their placid bay.

As he ate his breakfast, the doctor sneaked glances at Jewel as she began cleaning up the breakfast mess. She was tall, a couple of inches taller than the doctor, fully proportioned, brown-eyed, and always generous with a sly smile. He loved her ass the best, although he would admit that only to himself. Jewel, he guessed, knew—God knows she had caught him ogling her enough times over the past couple of years—but neither of them spoke of it. There were many obvious reasons for their silent denial. The doctor, for one, was in no position to pursue any sort of romantic relationship, or even a flirtatious one, for that matter. Three wives were more than enough for any one man, and he knew well enough by now at the age of sixty-four that his inability to get over Annie would most certainly, as it had done twice before, condemn any new alliance to ultimate failure. From Jewel's standpoint, the doctor surmised, he was nothing more than a grumpy old white man twice her age who was too old and too opiate-addicted to do much more than gawk even if he wanted to, which the doctor had to admit he often did. Besides she was in love with an itinerant blues singer named Gabriel White who made infrequent visits to Port St. Joe and over whom Jewel was clearly agog. Not to mention the plain fact, with the doctor as pale as the inside of an Apalachicola oyster and Jewel a darker shade of tupelo honey, that any sort of sexual dalliance on their part would amount to a felony crime in Florida—a certainty that was not to be disregarded either in the eyes of the law or of the Southern gentility on which each of their well-beings was dependent. That the doctor had given it this much thought was, of course, evidence of how much he cared about Jewel and just how much of his youthful romanticism still endured despite his dubious history and finite future.

The doctor finished his breakfast in silence as Jewel scrubbed and dried the cooking utensils and began wiping down the counter with a ragged dish cloth. He fantasized a moment about easing up behind her and wrapping his arms around her aproned waist, but instead he grabbed his black bag and headed for the back door.

"Put your dishes in the sink, Doc," Jewel instructed him like a long-suffering housewife.

"Yes, Jewel," the doctor muttered and headed out the back door, ignoring her request and abandoning the dirty dishes on the kitchen table. Despite the bang of the screen door slamming behind him and his diminished hearing, he was sure he heard her curse him.

Chapter Two

Dr. Berber drove his four-year-old, black, Model B Ford sedan through downtown Port St. Joe to his office on Reid Avenue. The little town seemed always to be living under a cloud, suffering one disaster after another, although the sun was shining so brilliantly this morning that it hurt his eyes. A cool, low-tide breeze blew in from the bay, bringing in the dank odor of sun-burnt salt marsh and decaying fish. As he drove past the new Port Theater just now nearing completion across the street from his office, he waved to Mrs. Collier, sweeping the sidewalk in front of her department store. Last year he had diagnosed her fifteen-year-old unmarried daughter Christine's chronic stomach upsets as a simple case of pregnancy, which prompted her being shipped off for a few months "to take care of a sickly aunt in Pensacola." Her boyfriend had suddenly quit high school and joined the army before Hank Collier, the girl's surly father, could unload his shotgun on him. Shortly thereafter, the mother, now bending over to pick up some speck of debris from the sidewalk, had developed a nervous condition that brought her to a complete state of wakefulness every morning at precisely 3:33 A.M. and would not allow her to return to sleep for the rest of the night. The doctor had suggested that she stay up later and, failing that, to just get up at 3:33 A.M. and enjoy a longer day. When neither of these solutions satisfied Mrs. Collier, he had given her a prescription for an alcohol-infused passionflower concoction called Passiflora, which seemed to do the trick.

Although the doctor was relatively content in the little town and expected to live out his few remaining days there, other townsfolk were not so satisfied. Some of the more sacrosanct went so far as to claim the town was cursed and that its misfortunes were actually God's retribution for the wayward ways of its citizenry. The right Reverend Garner Babcock Jr. for one. When he wasn't condemning them for their current shortcomings, he liked to regale his congregation from the pulpit of the First Baptist Church down on Third Street, as well as the doctor when he visited him for the treatment of the painful plantar warts on the sole of his right foot, about the evil deeds of their ancestors as far back as one hundred years ago. According to the reverend, who was an amateur historian, by 1838, exactly one century before to be precise, the bustling town of St. Joseph, as it was named then, boasted a thriving population of 12,000, making it the largest city in the new territory. The reverend exclaimed that it was a wealthy city that was home to one of America's first newspapers, the St. Joseph *Telegraph*, Florida's first railroad, the Lake Wimico and St. Joseph Canal and Railroad Company, connecting nearby Lake Wimico to St. Joseph's thriving port that he said rivaled those of Savannah, Charleston, and New Orleans. Long wharfs and piers extended well out into St. Joseph Bay where a forest of spars and masts crowded the harbor filled with vessels carrying away up to 150,000 bales of cotton annually. The town's rich cotton growers and shipping magnates built impressive mansions prefabricated by Northeast contractors, as well as sturdy brick offices and imposing warehouses. Pleasure cruises bound for New Orleans stopped in the city to allow passengers to hunt black bear, fish, or even gamble at one of the country's first thoroughbred race tracks. The city's extravagant parties, beautiful women, and brandy served over ice provided further affirmation of not only St. Joseph's wealth, but also its wickedness, the pastor preached. So prosperous was the booming city that it was selected, instead of Tallahassee, as the site of Florida's Constitutional Convention in 1838. Working from December 3, 1838, until January 11, 1839, the delegates drafted Florida's first constitution, but the Territorial Legislative Council rejected their document as being too liberal—another sign of the town's depravity, the preacher declared—and the issue of statehood was deferred until 1845, when Florida finally became America's twenty-seventh state.

While the doctor applied another layer of salicylic acid to the bottom of Reverend Babcock's big, ugly foot, he listened politely to the man's exhortations, wondering if the warts' pain had somehow shot up the reverend's body and tainted his brain. Since the doctor was a scientist, he did not adhere to the reverend's firmly held belief that subsequent events in St. Joseph were God's punishment for the early city's rampant decadence. But if pressed to give a spiritual explanation for the town's troubles, the doctor would have instead owed it to the town's loss of soul when, according to his best friend, Gator Mica, in 1839 shortly after the close of the Constitutional Convention, town officials expelled the two hundred remaining local American Indians and sent them on a forced migration to the distant Indian Territory in Oklahoma. That was the day old St. Joseph died, the doctor suspected, the day that the Great Spirit turned his back on the town and followed its ragged subjects westward out of their native land, leaving the remaining white residents to their fate.

Reverend Babcock took great relish in detailing the town's comeuppance. He said it began in August of 1841, when the crew of a ship from South America landed in the port of St. Joseph to bury their captain, who had died of yellow fever on the voyage. Within a few weeks, about three-quarters of the city's residents were also dead from the fever. Panic-stricken survivors abandoned their homes and fled. Ships steered clear of the port. Businesses were closed and shuttered. Then on September 14 of that same year, as if God's wrath could still not be assuaged, a disastrous hurricane struck the town, followed by fires that swept through the area later in the fall, leaving very little for the few hardy souls who later returned to the town only to be met with still another massive hurricane on September 8, 1844. For two days the winds increased, a lull settled, the winds shifted, and the storm hit with full force. Huge waves rushed inland and flooded what little was left of the city. Vacant buildings were blown to bits. And the sea—God, according to Reverend Babcock; the Great Spirit, per the doctor—claimed old St. Joseph. Today, the doctor often drove by the original site, less than five miles east of the new Port St. Joe, where he saw nothing but a jungle of pines, matted creepers, and palmettos—a sullen, unimpressive reminder of a once-thriving city now all but forgotten, except, of course, in one of Reverend Babcock's frequent, fervent sermons or an occasional tirade on one of his regular visits to the doctor's office, which the doctor understood were as much about saving the doctor's soul as curing the reverend's stubborn warts.

The doctor's office was Spartan, a model of spare, simple efficiency, the doctor thought: a little, square reception room with two oak chairs and an over-stuffed couch and a simple desk for Nadyne Wakefield, his nurse/receptionist; a door from the reception area to a narrow hall with four rooms off it—a toilet and an examination room on one side and his cramped office and an emergency operating room on the other—all painted white and bright, veiling its former use as the home of a wholesale seafood outlet. Not too bad for a little town of just 850 people. It wasn't a hospital, the nearest one being thirty miles northwest in Panama City, but it was fairly well equipped for a town this size. The doctor still owed on a lot of it, but it really didn't matter that much to him. Just as long as he could make the monthly rent on this place, pay his notes on the operating room equipment, his Ford, and his modest house, and, of course, pay Nadyne and Jewel a little something, he was able to hang on.

Unfortunately, during the past few years, during this awful Depression, he found himself all too often clinging precariously close to the edge. Many of his patients couldn't afford to pay and he wouldn't, couldn't refuse them care when they needed it. He was the only medical game in town, so he did the best he could and tried to scrimp by. Some people paid as Mrs. Wingate had, in strawberries, fruits, vegetables, whatever was ripe in their gardens; others in what little they had to offer: gasoline, insurance, venison, firewood, fresh fish, milk, and eggs. He had found the shingles that had blown off his roof in a storm replaced a few weeks ago. Even his banker, Clive Peters, whose daughter the doctor had delivered two years before, realized the special nature of the community's dependence on him and was therefore not loath to overlook, if necessary, a few weeks' tardiness on one of the doctor's loan payments.

"What do we have today?" the doctor asked Nadyne as he entered the office.

"Not too much," she reported, pushing her wire-rimmed spectacles up on her nose as she looked up from her open appointment book. "Follow-up on the Walker boy's hookworm in a few minutes. Mrs. Hardy for her monthly prenatal checkup at ten. Mrs. Lockhart asked if you could drop by sometime today and check on her father. He's not eating, she says. Liz Wright called from her mom's house and says she needs to see you this afternoon. Wouldn't say why. Then while you're out you need to check on Gus Moriarty too. Minnie says he's been running a fever and she doesn't think his arm is healing right. And Gator Mica has been around already this morning and says he wants you to go fishing with him this evening. I told him that he'd have to talk to *you* about that."

"Okay, send the Walker kid in when he gets here," the doctor instructed. "You okay today, Nadyne? You look a little down."

"I'm all right, doctor. Just old and tired, I guess."

"I know how you feel," the doctor sighed.

Nadyne Wakefield had been with him since he had moved to Port St. Joe three years earlier. She was a stout practical nurse and woman of indeterminate middle age who was born and raised in Port St. Joe, the only daughter in a family of four boys, all of whom had followed their father into the shrimping business. Luckily for Nadyne, women were not permitted on the fishing boats, so, at her mother's insistence, she was able to escape Port St. Joe, if only briefly, to attend nursing school at Florida State University in Tallahassee. She had returned a much more worldly and confident girl, but she remained shy and a just a bit too frumpy to attract a husband. So instead of raising a family, she had devoted herself to serving her neighbors as the town's only medical provider, until the doctor had relocated from Lynn Haven City in nearby Bay County. Despite her reserve, she knew nearly everyone in town, including their medical histories, so she had made the doctor's transition to Port St. Joe relatively painless. More importantly, she was organizationally astute, maintaining the office's financial and billing records, as well as keeping the doctor's appointments and house calls arranged so the doctor did not have to worry much about anything except keeping the town as healthy as he could.

But even with Nadyne's help, it seemed a challenge most of the time. Since the town had been reestablished as Port St. Joe in 1909, it had grown slowly but steadily as a timber and fishing center, but, as if the Great Spirit had not yet forgiven or forgotten the town's transgressions, the Great Depression continued pushing Port St. Joe into another spiral of misfortune. Much of the area's forests was now wasteland and most of the lumber mills had closed down after so many years of cutting and recutting of the surrounding timberlands. With little else besides hunting and fishing to sustain them, the few remaining people of the town became poorer and poorer, and sicker and sicker. The low-lying swamp land around the town bred mosquitoes as big as bats and as plentiful as sunshine and they carried a devastating variety of mosquito-borne diseases such as malaria, encephalitis, and yellow fever. Poor people on unhealthy diets were also particularly susceptible to tuberculosis, pellagra, and rheumatic fever. The doctor had also treated cases of polio and syphilis recently, not to mention the usual automobile, boating, and hunting accidents that struck arbitrarily without regard to financial or social position.

Despite his half-held belief in the Indian god's animosity, the doctor was ordinarily not a superstitious man, but he nevertheless hoped that the signing of an official peace treaty between the United States government and the few remaining Seminole holdouts in 1934, after over a century of "war," would finally appease the Great Spirit, and that the opening of the new St. Joe Paper Company would mark the beginning of a new, more prosperous time for this afflicted little village by the bay.

Chapter Three

The doctor's hope proved to be short-lived. At about 2:30 that afternoon, back in his office after making house calls, he received a long-distant telephone call from Sheriff Batson in the county seat in Wewahitchka, or Wewa as it was called by most natives in the area, about fifteen miles north of Port St. Joe.

"Doctor," the sheriff began, his voice uncharacteristically shaky. "I got some bad news. I just got off the phone with Harvey Winn out at the Cape San Blas Lighthouse. His assistant, young fellow named Martin, you might know him, has been killed. Harvey sounded awful upset, so I'm not sure yet exactly what happened, but apparently there's blood everywhere and Martin has been pretty well hacked up. That's what Harvey said anyway."

"What can I do?" the doctor asked.

"Well, listen, I'm going to go get Judge Denton and head out there," the sheriff said. "But could you leave now and drive over there just in case there's any life left in him or someone else has been hurt. You're about a half hour closer than I am by the time I round up the judge, so if you could check it out, Denton and me'll be there shortly. Okay?"

"You got it, Sheriff. See you there."

The doctor pushed the old Ford as fast as it could go along Constitution Drive south out of Port St. Joe along the bay and then turned right about seven miles out of town onto Cape San Blas, a narrow strip of white-sand peninsula that barely separated the quiet bay on the northeast from the wide expanse of the Gulf of Mexico on the southwest. Like a skinny fifteen-mile-long arm, the cape extended west from the mainland for about three miles and then abruptly jutted northward, paralleling that section of the Florida panhandle. At the arm's elbow stood the Cape San Blas Light, a white cast-iron skeleton tower enclosing a stair cylinder and topped with a circular black lens house about a hundred feet above the water. The light was lit with incandescent oil lamps and was placed here on one of the most desolate beaches the doctor had ever seen to warn ships off the shallow shoals that extended four or five miles out from the coast. The doctor remembered that a Coast Guard captain whose crushed hand he had once treated had told him the light was visible about ten miles out, so it was useful only to local fishermen, but offered no protection at all to the big cargo vessels that sailed from the Dry Tortugas to New Orleans in the main shipping lane about twenty miles out to sea. The tower was planted about half a mile off the main cape road in a field of dark-green sea grapes, sandspurs, and waving sea oats, with two stark, white cottages sitting nearby, one for the lighthouse keeper's family and the other for his assistant's family. They were nearly identical two-story bungalows with wide, tin-roof-covered porches extending out from the houses on three sides, making them look much larger than they actually were. There was a flourishing shared vegetable garden and listing chicken coop in the back, and, of course, the usual white-washed outhouses standing as silent sentinels where the flat flood plain gave way to a ragged grove of scrub oaks, palmettos, and dwarf longleaf pines.

The sheriff's description of the tragedy did not adequately prepare the doctor for what he found when he reached the lighthouse. The head lighthouse keeper, a slim, serious-looking, middle-aged man, came out to the doctor's car with a slight limp to greet him glumly. He introduced himself as James Harvey Winn and then led the doctor, black leather bag in hand, to a modest, brick shed behind the smaller of the two cottages, the assistant keeper's house, the doctor assumed. There, inside the shed, he found a bloody mess: the corpse covered with blood lying face up on a hard concrete floor, its dead eyes staring blankly at the ceiling above, a blood-encrusted hatchet and pen knife lying a few feet away. When the doctor tried to check for a pulse he discovered that the man's left wrist, entrails now exposed, had been severed all the way to the bone. Another large gash extended across his neck just below the chin with blood from the severed juggler vein dark and deep, clogging the man's open windpipe. When the doctor unbuttoned and opened the poor man's blood-soaked shirt, he found a hairy chest permeated with deep, gaping bloody holes. The doctor fought off nausea. He had treated some pretty nasty lacerations in his life, what with a variety of sawmill, farm machinery, and fishing accidents, even an alligator attack last year, but this was way beyond anything he had seen before. The body was already stiff and the brown blood was beginning to coagulate everywhere. The doctor guessed that he had been butchered about six or seven hours before, around mid-morning. But there was nothing he could do for him now.

"Anyone else hurt?" the doctor asked the lighthouse keeper, who was waiting outside the shed's door, smoking his pipe that smelled vaguely like the Prince Albert tobacco that the doctor's father used to smoke.

"No, everybody's okay. Though you might wanna check on Sally, that's Mrs. Martin, and her kids. They're pretty shook up."

The doctor stopped at a well behind the shed and pumped cold water on his blood-covered hands, scrubbing away the mess the best he could with a piece of gauze from his bag. He then crossed the sandy yard, climbed the porch steps, and tapped gently on the assistant lighthouse keeper's front door. He was no more prepared for the site of Mrs. Martin, strikingly alive and attractive, than he was for the gruesome torpor of her husband's mutilated corpse. Even with a tear-stained face and ill-fitting gingham shift, the widow took the doctor's words away for a moment, before he finally managed to mutter something that he hoped was in some way consoling.

She invited him in for tea, and he tried not to stare at her blood-shot green eyes and curly red hair as they sat across from one another at the kitchen table, sipping from their cups.

"Your children?" he finally asked. "How are they?"

"They're in their rooms now," she said. "The boys—John is twelve now and Ronald's six. All of them been crying all afternoon. The girls too—Earlene, she's thirteen, and Roseanne, poor baby, she's only seven, and she had to be the one to find Earl. She was home from school today, not feeling well, and I sent her out to the workshop to fetch him at noon when he didn't show up for dinner. I wish now I hadn't, that I'd gone myself, but . . ." She stopped and wept quietly. After a while she said, "I don't know what we're going to do now."

"Mrs. Martin, do you have any idea what happened to your husband?" the doctor asked.

"No. He went out to his workshop at around ten after he got finished tending the light, like he usually does, and I didn't hear a peep out of him the rest of the morning. I don't know. I just don't understand. He's been under a lot of pressure lately, financially. We've got a lot of debt. What with four kids and a pretty low salary. I'm not complaining. I know there're a lot of folks who are worse off than us. We should be thankful. At least he's got a job—or did. But he let it get to him. He would get down and was always scheming on how to catch up. We've got an insurance policy from the government, so I'm thinking maybe Earl killed himself so the kids and I could somehow get ahead. But, like I said, I don't know. I'm just so tired and confused right now I don't know what to think." And the tears began to flow again.

The doctor was seldom confident of his bedside manner, so he was not sure what to do next, but he was perceptive enough to recognize that she needed to be comforted and, by this time, so did he. There came upon him a sudden urge to hug her, so—spontaneously—he did. He bent beside her chair and awkwardly held her against his chest. At first, their bodies did not align, but the embrace nevertheless seemed to be soothing for both of them, and she soon stopped crying as he held her more tightly and gently touched the thick, soft coils of her hair. And, after a while, the doctor found himself surprisingly and curiously content. It was only a scant moment in time, he realized, but he instinctively knew that it was a meaningful one, the import of which he would ponder later. Now, he just wanted to hold her.

He was not sure how long they remained together like that, but all too soon he heard a car pull up outside and he knew that the sheriff must have arrived. He clumsily excused himself and went out to find Sheriff Batson, plucky as a cock, and Judge Denton, arrow straight and stiff, who were already marching toward the shed at the back of the house. The doctor was in no hurry to return to that bloody room, so he watched the two officials enter the workshop by themselves while he walked over to join the lighthouse keeper who was sitting in a rocking chair on his front porch, still smoking his pipe.

"Mind if I join you?" the doctor asked, as he climbed the stairs to the sagging porch. As he did so, he noticed a clump of dried blood that had stained the sole of his right shoe and wondered if Mrs. Martin had seen it. God forbid that he had tracked it across her kitchen floor.

"No, not atall," the keeper answered, gesturing to the empty rocking chair next to him. "I don't blame you for not wanting to go back in there again. Not for me neither. I've seen enough. Seen a lot worse in the war—got a bum leg to prove it—but it still ain't a pretty sight. How about you, you in the war?"

"No," the doctor said, "by the time I registered in 1918, I was too old. What do you figure happened out there in the shed?"

"Not sure. At first I thought it was suicide. When I went back there with Sally, Mrs. Martin, and my wife, Sally threw her arms around him and said something like 'Oh, darling, why did you do it?' and I got the idea in my head that he'd killed himself, but after looking at him I have a hard time believing someone could do that much damage to himself. What do you think?"

"I'd say you're right," the doctor said. "Maybe one or two cuts, but I counted fourteen all told, not something someone would or could do to himself. Anybody so angry with the man that he'd do something like that?"

"Not that I know of. Earl was no angel, mind you. He owed a lot of people. Had some gambling debts. Drank more than he should of. But I don't know anybody who'd want to kill him."

"How long you been the keeper out here?" the doctor asked.

"'Bout five years now, I guess. It's a lonely goddamn place. I guess you've heard the stories about it being cursed?

"No, can't say as I have."

"Folks in the service, the lighthouse service, say it's a hard luck station. Some say it's haunted. Damn tower's been blown over or washed away more times than you can count. During the Civil War, they say Confederate troops burned everything, including the keepers' cottages, 'cause they thought the light was helping Union warships. That was after one of them, the USS *Kingfisher,* landed here in 1862 and destroyed a big Confederate salt works right down the road a piece from here. One chief, not too smart a fellow, a few years back tried to shoot a hole through a railroad iron and the bullet ricocheted off it and killed him dead. Folks around here also talk about two twin girls apparently drowned while swimming; their clothes were found on the beach right down there, but their bodies were never seen again. 'Nother little girl got accidentally run over by another lighthouse keeper. Couple of other guys fell off the tower over there when they were trying to paint it. And just before me, back in thirty-two, a keeper name of Ray Hinton, shot himself to death right here no more than ten feet from where we're sitting. Yeah, I'd have to agree with them that thinks this here's a hard luck place. Don't know about it being haunted, but it sure ain't been good to a lot of people."

"Sure ain't," the doctor had to agree.

Chapter Four

So if it wasn't bad enough that the town was somehow ill-fated, the doctor thought as he drove back into town, but the lighthouse had to lie under the same ominous spell as well. Apparently the gods were not so easily appeased. He also thought about Sally Martin, the dead man's widow, whose image he couldn't seem to get out of his head. He was trying to figure out whether he just felt sorry for her or if there was something more to their brief embrace. There was no doubt that she was a beautiful woman and that he felt a certain tenderness toward her—a warm pleasure that he had not felt for a long time. It could probably be accounted for by his prolonged loneliness or an extended dearth of any meaningful physical contact, but regardless, it left him somehow unsettled and wanting badly to see her again soon, under more pleasant, conventional circumstances.

He drove directly home—to his cozy, comfortable old Victorian. Even though it was small, it had more space than the doctor really needed, a bath and two bedrooms upstairs and a parlor, dining room, and kitchen downstairs. There was a wide porch in front of the house, facing Long Avenue, but he seldom used it. Instead, he spent most of his time on the screened-in porch in back, facing his driveway and an alley and shaded year-round by a large, leafy live oak dripping serenely with Spanish moss. It was there on the back porch where he found Jewel, sitting in a wicker rocking chair, shelling a bowl of new peas and talking with her son Marcus. Her usual routine after taking Marcus to school and preparing the doctor's breakfast was to do the cleaning and laundry around his house, do whatever grocery shopping needed to be done for the both of them, check on her mother in the house she and Marcus shared with her in North Port St. Joe, and then pick up Marcus at school in the midafternoon. Then she would sometimes take Marcus back to her house for the evening, leaving something in the icebox for the doctor to warm up for supper when he got home or more often than not bring Marcus back to the doctor's house after school where Jewel, while Marcus was doing his homework, would cook an early supper for the three of them. It looked like it would be the three of them tonight.

"What's cooking?" the doctor asked, as he came up the back porch stairs.

"These here are English peas from Mary Lockhart's garden that she brought by a couple of hours ago," Jewel said, "and I'll fry up some potatoes, and—surprise, surprise—Gator Mica, lookin' for you to go fishin' with him, brought over some of them plump Bay Bayou oysters of his, so I told Gator that if he'd come back for supper I'd bake 'em up the way he likes 'em, you know, with onions and mushrooms and shrimp in that wine broth and all baked with bread crumbs on top. So Gator took off to get some shrimp and mushrooms. We got the rest. And, oh yeah, for dessert I got some shortnin' bread cookin' in the oven to go with the rest of them strawberries you had this mornin.' It's gonna taste so good it'll make your tongue fly up and slap your brains out."

"Well, Jesus, I hope not. Where do you come up with these things,

Jewel? You got some sort of weird Southern colloquialisms dictionary or something?"

"Mama, of course. Everybody knows she knows how to talk Southern better than a country congressman."

"Well, sometimes I feel like y'all are speaking another language. How's my little man, Mr. Marcus, this evening?"

"I'm fine, Doctor Berber," Marcus answered politely as always, looking up from the book on his lap. "How was your day?"

"You don't wanna know. Not Port St. Joe's finest, I'm afraid."

The doctor went inside so he wouldn't have to explain to the boy what had happened out at the Cape San Blas Lighthouse. He also needed to take off his blood-stained shoes, change out of his wool suit and tie, take an early dose of morphine, and relax alone a little bit before Gator showed up and the evening took on the unpredictable aspect that usually accompanied a visit from his best friend and favorite fishing buddy.

The doctor had met Abraham "Gator" Mica a couple of years ago when Gator had knocked on his door in the middle of the night looking like he had been in a brawl, which, as it turned out, he had. Fortunately, the doctor was able to patch him up without too much trouble, but his opponent had not fared as well; he had died, badly beaten, on the grimy floor of the Indian Pass Raw Bar. The sheriff had arrived to arrest Gator just as the doctor was applying the last of his bandages. For some reason, the doctor had taken an instant liking to his patient. Maybe it was the relaxed, straightforward way he had of facing the world. Or maybe it was his simple, earthbound style of living. One thing for sure was that there was not an ounce of pretension surrounding Gator Mica, and the doctor appreciated this in a world that, it seemed to him, was all too often overflowing with artifice. So with the help of a lawyer named Bob Huggins, who owed the doctor for some forensic work he had done several months before, Judge Denton had found Gator not guilty by reason of self defense. Finding enough witnesses who were willing to admit their presence at the fight or who were sober enough to remember it later had been a chore, but the doctor and Huggins had eventually found two men who were willing to testify that Gator's adversary had bated Gator by calling him a half-breed, which he was, and a son of a Injun-loving bitch, which Gator rather too vehemently denied. Fortunately for Gator, calling anyone a son of a bitch, Injun-loving or not, was emphatically frowned upon by Judge Denton, so Gator was acquitted.

In reality, Gator was the son of a white woman named Eliza Clinton and a Seminole father named Holata Mica, also known as the "Alligator King," who was reputed to be the last of the Seminole chiefs to be moved from Florida to Indian Territory in Oklahoma. The chief had managed to hide in the Everglades for some time, according to Gator, but government agents eventually caught up with him and convinced him that he would be paid a substantial sum of money if he emigrated west. He finally did so in 1858 and later served as a captain in the Union Army during the Civil War, but was never paid a dime for his land in Florida or for being relocated to Oklahoma. There, in 1887, Holata Mica's wife bore a son, Abraham, later to be nicknamed Gator after his father and for his considerable skill in gathering alligator hides. The boy listened intently to his father's stories about his homeland in Florida, and when he was just sixteen, he left the reservation in Oklahoma, which both he and his father despised, and made his way to his father's birthplace in the Everglades of south Florida. There he lived in the swamps and fended the best he could for himself. Both of Gator's parents were now long since dead, but the stories of his father's courage and long-standing intransigence were well known in the area, as were the tales of his son's outdoorsman skills, as well as his inherited impudence and reluctance to back down from any man.

When Congress authorized the creation of a new national park in the Everglades in 1934, Gator moved northward, eventually ending up in

the swamps and palmetto forests around Port St. Joe. There, near Indian
Pass, he built a little fishing camp and hunted, fished, trapped, gardened,
living mostly off the land and sea, and sold alligator hides or otter pelts
when he needed cash for gasoline, moonshine, and other provisions that
he couldn't catch, shoot, or grow. As the Depression deepened, there were
others who were forced into the mosquito-infested woods to survive, but
none were as successful at it as Gator, and few actually preferred this
precarious way of life as Gator had for the better part of the last thirty-five
years.

After Gator had been released from jail, he had made it a point to
repay the doctor by bringing something by the doctor's house at least
once a week, vegetables from his garden, amberjack or pompano that
he had caught in the Gulf, venison and duck in season, and scallops and
oysters from the shallow waters of his front yard . Sensing that the doctor
needed occasionally to escape the straight-laced confines of the provincial
little city, Gator began inviting the doctor to go fishing and hunting
with him. Gator not only knew the best fishing holes in the county, but
he also knew where and when to find deer, wild turkeys, and rabbits.
More importantly, Gator was a good listener, and when they were sitting
together in Gator's narrow little glade skiff on Lake Wimico, waiting for
a bite from a bass or bream, they would share their troubles. And since
Gator was pretty much a recluse, except for occasional nights out at the
Indian Pass Raw Bar, the doctor never had to worry about Gator telling
anyone else about whatever small town secret he might share with him.
In short, they became unlikely friends: an aging, small-town doctor and a
contrary, half-breed swamp dog. Gator's debt to the doctor for patching
him up and hiring a lawyer had long since been paid, but Gator continued
to share his hardscrabble bounty and to accept now and then the doctor's
standing invitation to join him and Jewel for supper whenever he felt like
it.

There was no doubt when Gator had arrived, from his old truck's bald tires sliding to a long halt in the shell driveway, to the porch screen door slamming, Marcus's laughter, and finally to Jewel's delighted scream when Gator came up behind her and gave her a big hug and a kiss, liberties the doctor would think often enough of but was too timid to take himself. The doctor was drawn downstairs to the kitchen by all this commotion and the smell of the baking shortbread. There, he found Gator filling the room, his broad smile beaming, a big, sunburned man, with shoulders as wide as a garden gate, dressed as usual in dirty dungarees and a tattered T-shirt, his sweat-stained, straw cowboy hat covering most of his unruly black hair that uncoiled wildly in all directions down nearly to his shoulders like Medusa's angry snakes. As the doctor entered the steaming kitchen, Gator was playing magician, pulling from a big burlap bag sitting on the kitchen table a tin coffee can full of shrimp, a brown paper bag of wild mushrooms, and a Kerr Mason jar of moonshine.

"Hey, partner, what's up?"

"Not much, Gator. Good to see you. Thanks for all the food, as usual."

"No problem, partner, as long as the best and prettiest cook in Gulf County cooks them up for me, I'll keep comin' back with more."

"Shut yo' mouth, Gator Mica," Jewel said, bending over to peek into the oven. " 'Stead of talkin', start shuckin' them oysters and shellin' them shrimp. Doc, you make yo'self useful too, and clean and slice them mushrooms. And Marcus, y'all get yo'self in here and start settin' the table."

Everyone dutifully did what they were told. Gator first poured each of the adults a half glass of moonshine, and, after he had set the table, Marcus begged the doctor to play some records on his new Gramophone record player, so the doctor put on his favorites: Count Basie's "One O'Clock Jump," Robert Johnson's "Cross Road Blues" that Gabriel had recommended, and Jewel's favorite, Mahalia Jackson's "Peace in the Valley."

When supper was ready, the four of them sat around the kitchen table and feasted. The Bay Bayou oysters were sweet and delicious, with the seasoned bread crumbs providing a satisfying crunchy compliment to the onions, mushrooms, shrimp, and briny oysters. The fresh green peas were thoroughly steamed and salted with a generous pat of creamy butter. The sliced potatoes and onions were fried crispy on the outside, soft on the inside, like the doctor liked them, in real fatback bacon grease. And each piece of strawberry shortcake was topped with a fluffy, round dollop of fresh cream energetically whipped almost to butter by Jewel as they all sat around the table and watched in anticipation.

After supper, Jewel put Marcus to work in the kitchen cleaning up and doing the dishes. She took her apron off and threw it over a kitchen chair, and joined Gator and the doctor on the back porch, out of earshot from the boy. Over another half glass of moonshine for each of them, the doctor told them about the murder on Cape San Blas.

"It was a bloody goddamn mess, I'll tell you that. Any idea who could have done such a thing?" the doctor asked them.

"Beats me," Jewel said. "Lot of strange stuff go on out there, if you ask me. Who'd want to live way out there all by themselves anyway? Ain't normal. I know one thing, no colored folks'll work out there, that's for sure. They all afraid."

"Of what?" the doctor asked.

"Ain't you heard the stories. Somethin' bad's always happenin' out there. Place is haunted, if you ask me."

"This Martin fellow," Gator said, "I think I know the man. If he's the guy I'm thinking of, he's sort of like a regular out there at the Indian Pass Raw Bar. Likes to drink and gamble. My guess would be he got himself too deep in debt with the wrong people—people who maybe wanted to send home a message to some others who weren't keeping up with their payments."

"And who might those people be?" the doctor asked.

"Hell, who knows," said Gator, emptying his glass, "but I sure wouldn't want to owe 'em nothing."

Chapter Five

The next day was St. Patrick's Day, and the doctor, a bit hung over, dragged himself out of bed and paid house calls in the morning: Jed Murdock with a worsening case of emphysema that couldn't be contained unless the man quit his two-pack-a-day habit; eighty-one-year-old Silvie Tate, living with her overweight daughter and growing more demented by the day; and Julie Rush, who had nothing more than a bad case of the blues attributable primarily, the doctor was sure, to a constantly drunk husband and three dirty, misbehaved, little children. Divorce him, the doctor advised, and regain control of your kids.

He ate a corned beef and cabbage lunch at Dad's Grill and then returned to his office, where he gave Mickey Wayne's mother a bottle of cod liver oil to treat the poor child's rickets. Later, he listened to Raymond Owens's congested lungs and gave him a Mantoux tuberculin skin test that he would check in a couple of days. Liz Wright, the colored prostitute who had called the day before, finally showed up with bruises all over her face and a deep cut over her left eye. When the doctor asked her what had happened, she refused to tell him. This was disturbing to him. He knew that such mishaps were an occupational hazard, but he didn't like it and wished he could do something more than just sew her up.

"Nadyne," he asked his nurse, when the Wright woman had left, "what's up with that? I don't understand why she wouldn't tell us who beat her up. Why would she want to protect someone like that?"

"Who knows. Could be her pimp. Could be a drunk customer. Could be some kind of weirdo sexual sadist. And anyone of them might hurt her worse if she tells on him. Could be the person is powerful, like some kind of fat-cat politician or a judge or something. Someone who could make her life miserable if she snitched on him. I'm afraid she's not in a very enviable position any way you look at it."

"Well, I guess not, but I think we should do something."

"I'll call Chief Lane and let him know what's going on, but I doubt anything will come of it. To the police, a prostitute, and a colored one at that, getting beat up is no big deal, I'm afraid."

"Okay," the doctor said, but he thought to himself that there had to be someone in their serene little town who should be held accountable and he vowed to himself that he would do something—he didn't know what exactly—to find out who.

Later that afternoon, after the doctor had just arranged for Ronnie Smith to be transferred to the Panama City Hospital to permanently set a leg he had broken playing baseball at school, Nadyne knocked on his office door and told him that Sheriff Batson was there to see him.

"Tell him to come in," the doctor said.

Sheriff Byrd "Dog" Batson was a brawny, sandy-haired tough guy with an ex-boxer's flat nose and scarred eyebrow. He had been elected because of his reputation for toughness, gained as an amateur boxer in his youth, as well as his ability, as an infantryman, to survive the Second Battle of the Marne in World War I. It didn't hurt either that his family had once, before the Depression, owned one of the largest cotton and timber farms in north Florida. Despite his rough edges, people seemed to appreciate a war hero and a once-rich man's native son.

"Sheriff, how are you?" the doctor said, shaking the man's hand, as the little room filled with the sickly sweet odor of the sheriff's after shave lotion, some sort of bay rum concoction that was not at all pleasing to the doctor's nose.

"Well, Doctor, I have to admit that I've been better. This whole day's been one big, goddamn circus. They've got big shots running all over the place with the opening of that new mill, and everybody's upset over the death of that lighthouse keeper out on San Blas, and both your police chief here in Port St. Joe and me are short-handed, so, I gotta tell you, I'm not looking forward to tonight when you can bet your shillelagh that more than one goddamn mick is gonna get smashed and start fightin' and I'm gonna have to haul 'em in."

"Sit down, Sheriff, please, relax," the doctor said, pointing to a chair in front of his desk. "But the mill opening went okay, didn't it?"

"Yes, I'm relieved to say it did," the sheriff said as he slouched down in the chair. "We had Mrs. DuPont and a bunch of other folks over from Jacksonville. Local dignitaries. A big deal."

"You don't sound too enthused."

"Listen, Doctor, maybe you don't know. You're kinda new around here, but—how to put this delicately—these damn DuPonts they came down here from up north, Delaware, wherever, and they did nothing more than steal the land right out from under the noses of a bunch of us, my daddy included. When things took a nosedive down here in the twenties, what with the big land bust and hurricanes galore and then this damn Depression, people around here were hit hard—prices for cotton, timber, fish, everything went to hell in a hand basket. And when prices were at their lowest and people were the most desperate that's when these carpet-baggin' vultures came down here and bought up every piece of land they could find at just a few cents on the dollar. Had this grand scheme where they were gonna turn this whole area into some kind of goddamn Garden of Eden, saying they're gonna make Port St. Joe the model city of the South or some such nonsense. Land that had been in families for generations was scooped up in a matter of months. People just needed the money, and that's the one thing the DuPonts had plenty of. So they took a little bit of it and they bought up north Florida, hundreds of thousands of acres of land, railroads, phone companies, every sawmill in sight, the whole goddamn town of Port St. Joe. Talk about a land grab. And, you know, I don't mind a man making a buck, but they're talkin' about making things better for everybody. Bullshit! Don't piss on my leg and tell me it's rain. The only people they're making it better for are themselves. Built this big ol' monstrosity of a paper mill. Gonna put people back to work they say. I wanna see what kinda jobs. Rock hard labor for the most part. Nobody in suits 'cept those big wigs up in Jacksonville or Delaware countin' their money. Us down here workin' in their smelly plant like nigguhs, while they're dumpin' who knows what kind of chemicals into the bay.

"I tell you, doctor, they ruined my daddy sure as we're sittin' here. Bought up all his land, the only thing he really loved. They say he was never right after my mother absconded when I was a baby, but the farm somehow kept him going. That is until all the prices went to hell, and he couldn't afford even to pay the taxes. Then the DuPonts came down and bought him out, lock, stock, and barrel, and left him rotting away in a little house on Mexico Beach. He didn't last a year. Didn't know what to do with hisself. At the end, he just set there and stared out at the sea, like some sad, goddamn dope."

"I'm sorry, Sheriff."

"Well, I'm sorry too—about gettin' so carried away about all that—

but there's really nothin' to be sorry about now. What's done is done. The way of the world, big fish eatin' the little fish. But, you know, I'm glad I'm up in Wewa and not down here in Port St. Joe. My gut tells me that they're just gonna ruin this place, like they did my daddy, one way or the other, sooner or later."

"Well, I hope not," the doctor said. "People do need the work, no matter how tough it is, and it seems like this little town's already seen more than its share of bad luck."

"That's true, doctor, it sure as hell has, which brings me to why I'm here. Judge Denton wants us to put together some kind of a jury to look into this Martin death. You know, to decide for sure whether it was a suicide or murder and what exactly happened. So, after the mill opened this morning, I've been running around town asking a few folks to serve on it, and since you were one of the first on the scene and can speak firsthand to the extent of the man's wounds I'd like you to serve too."

"Sure, Sheriff, I guess I could do that. What exactly do I need to do?"

"Well, we're convening a meeting next Wednesday morning at nine-thirty at city hall to sort it all out. So if you could make that and, in the meantime, go out and take another look at that shed where we found him, that would help a lot. I took the axe and knife to get them checked for fingerprints, but I'd like someone to take a closer look at the blood stains and all before they clean it up. I told Harvey and Sally, Mrs. Martin, not to touch anything until we had a chance to investigate further. And, while you're at it, if you could talk to Mrs. Martin and Harvey just to see if they remember anything else that could help us, that would be good too. I don't expect we're going to find out much more than we already know, but people are funny sometimes, they get to rememberin' after the dust has settled and the sheriff's gone. Maybe, who knows, they'll feel more comfortable talking to you than to me. Besides, as I said, I got my plate full right now, what with the mill opening, all these beekeepers about to descend on Wewa for tupelo honey season, and now they've set next Tuesday as the date to try the guy who robbed ol' man Harlow a few weeks ago and I gotta get ready for that. So, doctor, any help you can give me would be much appreciated."

"All right, Sheriff, I'll do what I can. Depending on what other calamity strikes, I'll try to get out there in the next couple of days."

The truth was the doctor wasn't doing the sheriff any favor at all. He couldn't wait to see Sally Martin again.

Chapter Six

When the doctor arrived at the lighthouse late the next afternoon, he found Harvey Winn where he had left him two days before, sitting on his front porch in a rocking chair, smoking a pipe. The spring was already growing hot, and the doctor wiped the sweat from his forehead with his handkerchief as he approached the house. It was almost time to break out his seersucker suit, he thought. Even though he was wearing his blue, lightweight wool three-piece suit today, it was still too warm and even a bit snug. He was going to have to start watching his weight more closely or he wouldn't be able to fit into his summer clothes.

"Sheriff called and said you would be dropping by again," the lighthouse keeper said. "What can I do for you, Doc?"

"Well, the sheriff wanted me to take a look at the shed again, if you don't mind. And I wanted to ask if you had any more ideas about who might have had it in for Mr. Martin?"

"Well," the lighthouse keeper said, "I have been giving it some thought, and the only thing I can think of is that maybe someone's out to get our jobs. Other keepers said that they had got threats, so I'm thinkin' maybe someone is trying to get us out of here so they can get our jobs.

Scares me to death, if you wanna know. If they murdered Martin, then I might be next."

"Do you have any idea who these people might be?" the doctor asked.

"No, not really. Desperadoes. Lots of people 'round here need jobs, need money. Lots of desperate people out there."

"Hmm," the doctor said, thinking to himself that a little paranoia had apparently set in here. "You said the other day that Martin owed some people. Any idea who?"

"Not really. I know he liked to gamble. He told me that. Out there at the Indian Pass Raw Bar. But I never went out there with him, so I don't know much about who he might owe something to. Hard to say."

"You said he was a drinking man. Did he deal with any moonshiners as far as you know?" the doctor asked.

"Well, I suspect he did. He'd bring a jug around every now and again. Had to get it somewhere. Probably out there at Indian Pass, be my guess."

"Did he mention any names?'

"No, not that I recall."

"Mind if I take another look at that shed then?"

"Nope," the keeper said. "Help yourself. I haven't touched a thing."

There wasn't a cloud in the deep, endless azure sky. There was a slight breeze from the sea and it was eerily quiet as the doctor walked back to the shed. All he heard were the squalls of sea gulls and the refrain of waves breaking gently on the shore. By contrast, it was dark and cold and smelled of mold inside the shed, like a mausoleum. How appropriate, he thought. He found a long string connected to a naked light bulb on the ceiling and pulled it to light the cramped space. It couldn't have been more than five feet by twelve, he estimated. There was just the one door and no windows and a waist-high work bench extending the length of the longest wall. He wondered what they worked on in here—lighthouse equipment maintenance of some sort, household projects, general hiding out? Hung on long nails on the wall above the work bench were various tools: a hand saw, hammer, scythe, monkey wrench, and other gizmos the doctor didn't recognize. On the bench itself were only a whetstone at one end and a wool cap, Martin's he assumed, with a half-full pack of Chesterfield cigarettes still lying in it. On the gray concrete floor were a large blood-splattered tool chest and three pools of dried blood. One pool was connected to another, the largest, about two to three feet across, nearest the door, suggesting that Martin may have dragged himself across the floor to get to the door. There were also bloody fingerprints on the bench leg nearest the door, probably those of the dying man trying to pull himself to his feet. How much pain had he endured, the doctor wondered. The blood loss from the wounds on his wrist and neck must have been rather rapid, so he likely choked on his own blood or passed out from blood loss before suffering for too long. The doctor was kneeling down to get a closer look at the fingerprint stains when he sensed a shadow falling over him from the open door behind him. He froze, then jerked around suddenly to find himself face to hem with a blue cotton dress inches from his nose. He was sure he got a whiff of Ivory soap and arrowroot starch before he rose to look into the apprehensive, lightly freckled face of Sally Martin.

"Sorry I startled you. Did he suffer long?" she asked, as if reading the doctor's mind.

"No, not long. I believe he passed out rather quickly."

"Find anything interesting?" she asked.

"No, nothing new, at any rate. How are you?"

"I've been better. But we're surviving. That's about all I can say at this point."

"And the children?"

"They're having a hard time. Truth be told they didn't see that much of their daddy when he was alive, but he was theirs anyway. They haven't gone back to school yet, so they're inside now getting packed, I hope. Do you mind if we walk? It's such a nice day and I need to get out of the house for a while. They'll be fine on their own for a spell."

"Of course," the doctor said, pulling the string to extinguish the light. There really wasn't any more to learn in the gruesome little room. "Shall we walk on the beach?"

They trudged silently through the shifting sand, single-file, her leading the way, down the narrow path across the dunes carpeted with silver-leaved lupines, their blossoms weaving a blue crazy quilt of color across the bleached knoll. When they reached the wide, white sandy beach, they took their shoes and socks off and walked side by side a few feet from the breaking waves.

"So where are y'all packing for?" he asked when they had walked a few yards.

"The plan is to leave tomorrow for Dothan in Alabama. That's where Earl's family is. His folks and a brother and sister, some aunts and uncles live there. The body has already been shipped by rail. They have a family plot apparently. We're all driving up there for the funeral on Sunday afternoon. Then we'll return on Monday or Tuesday in time for me to testify on Wednesday for a jury they've put together."

"Yes, I'm afraid I've been recruited to be a part of that. How about your family? Are they in Dothan too?"

"No, I'm originally from West Texas, near Pampa. Earl and I met there when he was in the army. We had Earlene there and then Earl, 'cause he had some mechanics experience in the army, got this job here about twelve years ago now, and we've been here ever since. I'm an only child and my parents passed a few years back, my daddy of dust pneumonia and my mama of tuberculosis during the Dust Bowl."

"So sorry to hear that. You're planning to stay here then?" the doctor asked.

"I think so. Earl's family and I don't get on that well, and I'm used to it here now, and the kids have friends in school. Harvey said we could stay in the assistant keeper's house until the first of the year or until we can find something reasonable in town, so we have some time. Harvey's going to hire Johnny Jones to help out temporarily until they find somebody permanent. He lives in town and has filled in out here when we've needed him."

"Are you afraid?"

"Of being hurt, murdered? No, they had their chance. Of what's going to happen next, of life? Yes."

"If there's anything I can do to help, please let me know, anything," the doctor offered.

"Thank you," she said. "That's very kind of you. I'll need a job soon, so if you hear of anything. As I think I said the other day, Earl had a government life insurance policy for three thousand dollars that should get us by for a while, at least until I find something. So we should be okay."

They walked along together, without speaking, the sky beginning to redden as the sun began its silent slide into the Gulf of Mexico. He wanted badly to reach over and hold her hand, but he didn't want to be too bold. At some point—he wasn't sure how long they had been walking—she suggested that they better turn around and get back to the kids.

"You also said the other day that y'all had a lot of debt," the doctor said, as they skirted a beached jellyfish. "It's none of my business, but could that have anything to do with your husband's death, do you think?"

"That's a good question," she answered. "To be honest with you, I don't know who all we owe at this point. Earl kept a lot of secrets and was always surprising me with one new debt or another. I tried to keep track of it all, but Earl had a way of always spending more than we had. His uncle arranged a loan for us just before Earl was killed, but Earl was still worried. Before we got the loan, Earl said he had a plan, but he wouldn't tell me what it was. The truth is, Doctor Berber, that three-thousand-dollar insurance money may be all spent, for all I know."

The doctor didn't know quite where to go from there. He was a doctor, not a detective. So he just continued to walk along with her, as though they were two lovers out on a Sunday stroll, he thought. After a while, when the two cottages came back into sight, and, as if thinking it over and deciding that she trusted him or maybe just needing to confide in someone, she said, "Look, you might as well know the truth. Earl was not a very nice man. He drank and gambled away most of what we made. Harvey tended the light from around sunset until midnight and then Earl took over until sunup. Then he disappeared into his workshop until dinnertime and then he slept in the afternoon until dark. Then he got up and went out carousing. He never was mean or anything. He just wasn't around much. Like a lot of folks, we got married too young. I was just a kid—only eighteen. Earl was a few years older, but we were still too young. When we first came here it was all right for a few years, but then, to be honest, I think Earl just plain got bored. Can't blame him really. There's just not that much to do out here. So he started drinking and gambling with his buddies over there at the Indian Pass Raw Bar 'most every night and I stayed here and did the best I could to raise the children."

She began to cry and, as they walked behind a high dune that blocked their view of the keepers' cottages, he stopped and held her once again. Her hair smelled like gardenias and her body was warm, firm, and moist against his. "I often wished he was dead," she whispered, her lips brushing his ear, "but I didn't kill him."

The doctor believed her.

Chapter Seven

The following Wednesday morning turned out to be a dreary, gray, cloudy day. Dr. Berber filed into the windowless City Council chambers at Port St. Joe's City Hall, along with the other members of the so-called jury, who were instructed by a stern, gray-haired woman whom the doctor did not recognize, to sit at the long table usually reserved for City Councilmen. The imposing woman directed the witnesses to sit facing the jury table in the first row of oak chairs ordinarily used by the few citizens who attended the monthly meetings. Sally Martin was already seated there, dressed in a simple black dress, her hair pulled harshly back from her face, next to a freckled face girl he guessed to be about twelve or thirteen years old, who looked so much like Mrs. Martin that the doctor assumed she was her daughter. Next to them was Harvey Winn, his black hair slicked down and looking uncomfortable in a gray three-piece suit and wrinkled red tie. Eventually they were joined in the front row by Sheriff Batson, Julian Fleming, who was a local undertaker, and another man the doctor did not recognize. The remaining few chairs behind them filled up quickly with area newspaper reporters and some curious townspeople whom the doctor knew, as well as several strangers he did not.

As everyone was finding a place to sit, the doctor caught Sally Martin's eyes, and they exchanged a familiar smile. He thought she looked elegant dressed so formally stiff in her dark mourning clothes, and he wished that he were sitting closer to her.

Once everyone was packed into the little room, Judge Arthur Denton, rail-thin and hook-nosed in a blue serge suit, entered and set at the far end of the council table. He explained that since this was not an actual trial and since the City Hall was more convenient to most of the witnesses than his courtroom in Wewahitchka, Port St. Joe's mayor had generously allowed them to use this room for the hearing, the purpose of which, he said, was to determine the facts and circumstances surrounding the death of E. W. Martin one week ago today, on March 16, 1938.

"First off, let me make a few introductions," the judge continued in his high, nasal whine. "Seated here next to me are Ronald Benton, serving as this jury's foreman, as well as Lee Hardy, Dr. Van Berber, G. P. Barry, Joseph Donovan, and Charles Harrel. Also joining us today are William Johnson, Jr., and Harry Stanton of the U.S. government lighthouse service, as well as Marvin Williamson, a federal investigator.

"Our witnesses are seated here in the front row, and I'm going to call them one by one to be sworn in by the clerk and then to be seated in this chair to my right to address the jury and answer any questions that the jury and I might pose. As I said, this is not a trial. No one will be found guilty or not guilty today. So the usual courtroom rules will not apply.

"The court first calls James Harvey Winn, who is the head lighthouse keeper at the Cape San Blas Lighthouse."

After being sworn in, the keeper, wiping sweat from his brow with a dingy white handkerchief, was asked by Judge Denton to tell the jury what had happened last Wednesday.

"Well, me and my wife, Mary, and my daughter, Gloria, left for Port St. Joe for supplies at about nine that morning. We got back at about eleven-thirty. We were resting after dinner when, at about two-thirty, Mrs. Martin came to the house and said that their little daughter had found her father lying in the shed and that he was hurt and to go to him. My wife and I went with Mrs. Martin and saw her husband lying on the floor in a pool of blood with a hatchet and a knife near him. I noticed blood on his hand and lifted his wrist, and I saw it had been cut to the bone, but I saw no other wounds or any blood on his clothes. At that time I believed he was a suicide. I did not move the body, but went right away and telephoned the officials in Wewahitchka."

"What made you think it was a suicide?" Judge Denton asked in his sour, judicious voice.

"Well, like I said, at first I didn't notice any other wounds except for his wrist. Then, when we came into the shed, Mrs. Martin threw her arms around her husband and said, 'Oh darling, why did you do it?' As far as I know, she did not move the body. It was stiff and the blood was clotted. I picked up the knife without thinking when I first came in, but I put it back in exactly the position it was in when I first saw it, though I may have been excited and not gotten it exact.

"But I think Martin was actually murdered because of the manner and position of the wounds. He had always got along well with everybody, had no domestic troubles, and was in good spirits on the morning he was found dead."

Mr. Benton, the jury's foreman, then asked the keeper if he knew if Martin had any life insurance.

"I believe he had a three-thousand-dollar policy with the government," Winn said. "It's a standard part of our benefits with the lighthouse service."

"And do you know if there is a suicide clause in that policy?" Benton inquired. "A clause that says that the amount of the policy is not payable if the insured commits suicide?"

"No, not right off hand. I don't really know."

Then one of the lighthouse service men, Mr. Stanton, stood up and asked Judge Denton if he could speak. Judge Denton nodded for him to go ahead.

"Mr. Winn is correct. Martin was covered by a three-thousand-dollar life insurance policy through the lighthouse service, but just after the first of this year he elected to pay the extra premium and up the value of that policy to a total of twenty thousand dollars. And, yes, there is, in fact, a section of that policy which prohibits payment if it is proved that the insured committed suicide or was killed specifically for pecuniary gain."

"Pecuniary gain?" Benton asked.

"Yes, if he was killed by someone to collect the insurance amount."

The doctor looked at Sally Martin who was starring in disbelief at the government agent, apparently unaware that her husband had recently upped the value of his life insurance policy. This bit of new information seemed for a moment to stun not only the widow, but also everyone else in the room. But instead of an audible gasp, as there was in all those melodramatic courtroom moving pictures, there was a speechless, stupefied silence for several seconds.

"Thank you, Mr. Stanton, for clarifying that," Judge Denton finally said and turned his attention back to the witness. "Now, Mr. Winn, if Martin's death was not by his own hand, do you have any idea who might have killed him?"

The lighthouse keeper then went into the same story he had told the doctor last week, about what he called the unknown desperadoes who were out to get their jobs. When he'd heard enough, the judge cut him off and called the next witness.

Sheriff Batson, in his usual gray uniform and black Western boots, recounted Harvey Winn's telephone call and what he had found when he arrived at the lighthouse. He concluded his account by saying, "So I photographed the fingerprints on the hatchet and knife that were found next to the body, and I've sent the photos off to Washington to see if we can get a match on Mr. Martin's or Mr. Winn's prints, since they're on file there like all government employees, and to see if any other prints were on the weapons."

"Thank you, Sheriff," Judge Denton said. "The court now calls Dr. Van Berber to the witness chair."

The doctor then told about what he had found on his two visits to the lighthouse, and the judge asked him about his opinion on whether the death was a suicide or not.

"I don't believe it was suicide," the doctor said, purposely avoiding Sally Martin's eyes. "It would not be possible for a man to stab himself so many times and then practically cut his wrist in two, or for a man to cut his wrist so deeply and then stab and cut himself fourteen times in the chest and throat."

Julian Fleming, the portly, balding undertaker, was the next witness. Judge Denton asked him to describe the dead man's wounds.

"The man had one very deep cut on his left wrist, to the bone," Fleming said, sweating profusely. "Another long cut across the throat, practically ear to ear, again quite deep, two to three inches. There were twelve other very deep cuts across his chest, most into or near his heart. The cuts were so deep that when I pumped the embalming fluid into his veins it spurted out from three cuts on his chest and from the slash across his neck."

Sally Martin and her daughter were now in tears, and the judge called for a brief recess before calling the remaining witnesses. The doctor left the building to get some fresh air, but apparently Mrs. Martin remained in the council room since he didn't see her outside. Instead, he found himself huddled on the front steps, under the eaves of the gray granite City Hall, out of the light rain that was now falling, with a murmuring group of smoking men, conjecturing among themselves on what they had just heard and what it actually meant. The doctor kept to himself, thinking more of Sally Martin than how her husband had been killed. All this talk of suicide and death did not jibe at all with what he was feeling about this intriguing, pretty, young widow.

"The court now calls Clint Barnes," the judge announced when everyone was settled back into the claustrophobic little room. When the husky new witness was sworn in and seated, Judge Denton said, "Could you tell us, Mr. Barnes, your relation to the deceased?"

"Yes, your honor, I'm his uncle, his mother's brother."

"And what is your opinion on Mr. Martin's state of mind just prior to his death?"

"Well, I do not believe he committed suicide. The cuts on his body indicated to me that he had been murdered. No man living could stand to stab and cut himself so many times. He was the type of man who would not, in my opinion, do such a thing. It is true he owed some money, but I had arranged at the bank for him to receive a loan, so that could not have been a motive. He had no occasion to commit suicide. He just did not appear to be the type of man who would take his own life."

"Do you know who might have wanted him dead?" the judge asked.

"No. To my knowledge no one ever threatened him."

Judge Denton then called the final witness and said to her, "Thank you so much, Mrs. Martin, for you and your daughter joining us this morning. I know this must be hard for both of you, so just a few questions, if you don't mind. First, is there any reason that you know of, why your husband may have committed suicide?"

"No," she answered. "He had at times become depressed because of our financial problems, but he never talked about suicide or hurting himself. He was his usual self on that morning, before . . ."

"Do you know of anyone who may have wanted to harm him?" the judge asked.

"No. Earl was a very friendly man. As far as I know, he had no enemies."

"And finally, Mrs. Martin, did you know that your husband had increased the value of his life insurance policy?"

"No, I did not."

"Do you know why he may have done so?"

"No," she whispered and began weeping again.

Chapter Eight

Judge Denton then excused the witnesses and the spectators in the room and asked the jury to remain. After the public had been cleared, the judge asked each jury member to state his opinion on whether Martin's death was by his own hand or at the hands of someone else. While the fact that the man had so recently increased the value of his life insurance policy bothered everyone, the testimony of his uncle that a loan had been arranged seemed to mitigate Martin's immediate need for money and therefore his apparent motive for taking his own life. Besides, the man surely must have been aware of the suicide exclusion in the policy and, as everyone agreed, could not, in any case, have physically committed the damage that had been done to his own body.

After everyone stated their opinion and the tragedy had been discussed for more than an hour, with dinnertime rapidly approaching, Judge Denton asked if everyone agreed that Martin's death was caused by a party or parties unknown and that the sheriff should be instructed to find out as soon as possible who was responsible for what they now deemed to be a murder. One by one, as the judge polled them, all six jurors agreed.

The doctor was starving by the time the judge finally released them at around one o'clock. But just as he was getting in his car, a Port St. Joe police car pulled up and a patrolman yelled at the doctor to follow him out to the new paper mill, that an accident had occurred there. With a blasting siren and flashing lights, the patrol car sped through Port St. Joe with the doctor following as close behind as he and his old Ford could manage, windshield wipers working fiercely to clear the continuing rain.

When the doctor and the patrolman arrived at the front gate of the St. Joe Paper Company, they were directed to a door at the end of a long tall, tin building. A strange, sulphuric odor, like rotten cabbage or eggs, greeted them as they entered. Inside lay an unconscious man with a steel cable about an inch in diameter coiled snakelike around his chest. He was pale and unconscious but was still breathing, just barely and with some difficulty. One end of the thick cable was connected to a large winch on the ceiling above and the other to a pulley mechanism on the wall. The ensnarled man had somehow become trapped between the two.

"Is there any way to loosen the cable?" the doctor yelled to the men surrounding the dying man.

"No, when he got caught all the equipment seized up," one man answered. "The engine shut off automatically and we can't get it going again."

"Then find a cutting torch," the doctor instructed. "There has to be one around here somewhere. We've got to get this cable from around him or he'll die."

It seemed like it took forever, but a torch was finally found and, with some difficulty, the restricting cable was cut. Two of the men helped the doctor to slowly unwrap the stiff cable from around the man. His chest was crushed, but he somehow continued to breath. Several ribs were broken for sure, and the doctor hesitated to think what kind of internal injuries the poor man must be suffering. The best thing to do was to get him as quickly as possible into the intensive care unit at the hospital in Panama City where oxygen, x-rays, and assisted breathing apparatuses were all available.

The doctor supervised the six men who were recruited to lift the man as gently as possible off the concrete floor and into fire station's ambulance that he had called while the man was being cut loose. As he watched the ambulance and the police speed away, the doctor silently prayed, to whom he was not sure, that they made it to the hospital before it was too late.

While he was there at the new mill, a burly, mustached supervisor in canvas coveralls and steel-toe boots asked the doctor if he would take a look at another man who had also been injured earlier in the day. He found Richard Nichan, a dark-haired kid, maybe eighteen years old, operating a forklift truck that moved pine logs from a huge yard behind the mill onto a wide conveyer belt that carried them into the plant. The supervisor instructed the boy to turn off the forklift and show the doctor his injuries. The boy's right index finger was swollen and immobile, no doubt broken, and the outside of his right leg was red and badly scraped.

"What happened?" the doctor asked.

"A log fell off a pile over there and hit my hand and then caught my leg. I'll live, I reckon.'"

"Have you washed that leg?"

"Yes, sir."

"Go wash it again. Good this time, with soap and hot water."

"Yes, sir," the boy replied and limped off into the plant.

"Quite a day," the doctor said to the supervisor.

"Yeah, it's our first day of trial operations, so things are a little rough. It'll get better."

"I hope you're right," the doctor said.

When the boy returned, the doctor slathered the scrape in mercurochrome and wrapped it in a white gauze bandage. Then, using the end of a tongue depressor and adhesive tape, he set the boy's finger and told him to come to his office on Friday to make sure everything was healing okay, knowing full well he would never see the kid again unless something went terribly wrong.

As the doctor drove over to the Club Cafe for dinner, he thought for the first time about the host of new injuries and health problems this big new mill was just now starting to spawn, and he didn't know if he had the energy anymore to deal with them. His workload was now tolerable, but at his age he just didn't want to deal with any increased responsibilities. He was hoping to slow down a bit, in fact. It was getting so that he would much rather spend time fishing and hunting with Gator or just sitting around the house with Jewel reading and listening to music than tending to all the various ills of this little town. Truth was his birthday was coming up in a few days and he was feeling his age. Not to mention the fact that he had not yet had his midday morphine dose and he was growing increasingly tired and irritated.

Now, as he entered his office after dinner, he saw that relief was nowhere in sight. The little waiting room was full. He knew everyone there and what likely they were there for, except for the formal man sitting in the corner in his brown wool suit. It was one of the lighthouse service men who had been at the meeting this morning—what was his name? He was the one who had sprung the increased insurance policy value surprise that had so disturbed everyone and left an annoying question mark hanging over their heads.

"Mr. Stanton, Harry Stanton," the man stood up and extended his soft right hand. "I'm with the Granite State Life Insurance Company, the firm that provides life insurance for all lighthouse servicemen. I was at the meeting this morning. I was wondering if I might have a brief word with you before you start attending to your patients?"

"One moment, please.

"Nadyne," the doctor said, grabbing her arm and pulling her into the hallway. "Anything that can't wait out there?"

"No, the usual. The man's been here longer than most of them, so you might as well talk to him and get it over with."

"Okay, give me a couple of minutes and then send him in." The doctor hurried to his office, locked the door, and measured out the morphine. It had been a stressful morning, and it didn't look like the afternoon was going to be any better.

"What can I do for you, Mr. Stanton?" the doctor said when Nadyne had brought him back and seated him in front of the doctor's desk. He was a prissy little man, the doctor thought, sitting there, his paisley tie knotted perfectly, so straight and formal in his affected, officious way.

"Well, Doctor, I just wanted to ask you a couple of questions, if you don't mind. My job with Granite State is to investigate cases like this one where the insured passes away shortly after taking out a policy or increasing its value, as Mr. Martin did. And I understand your testimony this morning. It seems clear that Mr. Martin could not have inflicted all those wounds you described on himself, but was there anything else you observed or heard in your discussions with the widow or the head lighthouse keeper that might indicate something else was going on?"

"Something else?"

"Yes, that perhaps Mr. Martin was somehow attempting to take advantage of his situation?"

"His situation? What situation are you talking about, Mr. Stanton?"

"Well, it appears that Mr. Martin was in considerable debt and that the payment on this insurance policy, especially at such a high value, would hold particular advantage for his family."

"What exactly are you suggesting?"

"I'm not suggesting anything, sir. I'm just inquiring if you noticed anything that might indicate that Mr. Martin was not operating in the most honorable fashion."

"That he was defrauding your company?" the doctor asked. "Is that what you're suggesting?"

"Look, Doctor Berber, I don't know what's going on here, but something is not right. I've been doing this for nearly fourteen years now and I know when something is fishy, and, let me tell you, something is fishy here, that's for sure."

"What exactly, Mr. Stanton, do you mean by fishy?"

"I believe that Mr. Martin may have gotten himself and his family so far in debt that he decided to increase the value of his life insurance policy with my company and then hire someone to kill him."

"That's a pretty drastic step, wouldn't you say?" the doctor said. "Besides his uncle said this morning that he had arranged a loan, so why would he need to conspire to kill himself to pay his debts?"

"That's what I'm paid to find out, and that's why I'm here asking you if you might know anything that would help me answer that question."

"Well, Mr. Stanton, I wish I could help you. I really do, but I'm not a trained investigator like you. I'm a doctor with a waiting room full of impatient patients. So if you'll excuse me, it's time for me to do some doctoring now."

The doctor rose and opened the office door for his guest, indicating that their meeting was now at an end.

"Thank you for your time, Doctor," the insurance man said on his way out. "If you think of anything else, please don't hesitate to contact me. Here is my card and, for the next few days at least, I can be reached here in town at the Port Inn."

When the doctor got home that evening, later than usual, he was glad to see that Jewel and Marcus were still there. He needed to talk to someone about this strange, disturbing day, and Jewel was all too eager to hear what was happening. So, after they had finished Jewel's juicy pot roast, orange-glazed carrots, and mashed potatoes with thick brown gravy, and when Marcus was once again banished to the kitchen to clean up and wash the dishes, Jewel and the doctor sat on the screened-in porch and drank a little moonshine and watched the light rain as it continued to fall. The mist and the honeysuckle vine growing up the side of the porch smelled rich and spicy in the evening air, and the doctor realized that he ached all over as he sank into the soft cushions on the white wicker chair.

"So what do you think, Doc?" Jewel asked, when the doctor had finished telling her everything that had happened. "Do you think that insurance guy's right? Do you think somethin' fishy is goin' on?"

"You know, Jewel, I don't know. It's been a long day and I'm feeling awfully tired. He could be right for all I know. What do you think?"

"Oh, yeah, I'd say somethin' fishy goin' on all right. Smells about as fishy as St. Joseph Bay at low tide. And I betcha I'm gonna find out why. Just give me a couple of days."

"Jewel, what the hell are you talking about? Don't you dare get yourself involved in all this. There's a murderer out there someplace and you don't need to be messing with him."

"Don't you be worryin' about me, Doc," Jewel said with her familiar arch grin. "Just be worryin' about yo'self. You ain't got no dog in this fight. Get some rest. And Marcus, git yo'self out here and stop listenin' at the door. It's time to go."

And with that she and the boy were gone.

Chapter Nine

Two days later on Friday morning, Jewel, instead of fussing as usual at the sink, dried her hands on her apron and sat down at the kitchen table with the doctor as he ate his breakfast. She was dressed in a starched white blouse and light blue skirt. Her dark brown eyes sparkled as she filled their cups with black coffee and watched the doctor chew a big bite of cured ham.

"Good ham, Jewel. Where'd you get it?"

"Barbara Jones dropped it off yesterday afternoon. Might as well get used to it. It's at least a twenty-pounder. Smoked out at their place over a nice pecan fire, she said."

"Yes, I do believe they raise the best hogs in the county out there. Too bad they got so many kids—eight now, I believe, and the poor woman's expecting again—unlucky for them, they barely get by, but lucky for us, I guess, since we get paid with this tasty ham."

"Doc, I hate to interrupt yo' little revelry on Jones' smoked hog, but I got some news for you," Jewel said, as she sipped her coffee.

"Yes?"

"Well, you know Georgia Reeves. She's a waitress over at the restaurant in the Port Inn. Good friend of mine. Lives in the next block over. Brighter than a bee's bum. Well, it seems like at lunch yesterday she was serving the sheriff and that lighthouse insurance guy you told me about, and she heard some interestin' things."

"She was eavesdropping," the doctor said.

"Yes, exactly. You think us colored folks can't wait on y'all and listen at the same time? You want to hear this or not?"

"Go ahead."

"Well, this insurance fellow tells the sheriff that after he talked to you on Wednesday afternoon, he went out to the San Blas Lighthouse and talked to the widow and the lighthouse keeper—what's his name?"

"Winn, Harvey Winn."

"Yeah, that's him. So this insurance guy finds out from Winn and the widow that the dead guy used to hang out at the Indian Pass Raw Bar. So this insurance guy decides to go out there, and he tells the sheriff that people out there say the dead guy was the friend of this moonshiner man named Lucky. And this guy Lucky ain't been seen since the day the dead guy got dead. So the insurance guy is asking the sheriff about if he knows who this Lucky guy is and all. And Georgia said the sheriff said he didn't know no Lucky, but that he'd look into it."

"Georgia say anything else?" the doctor asked.

"No, not about that," Jewel thought for a moment. "Said she'd been havin' some trouble with her husband. He lost his job with the railroad and he's been drinkin' a lot. Oh yeah, and she said the sheriff scared her, and this insurance guy was a little squirrelly, if you know what I mean."

"Squirrelly?"

"Yeah, you know, not too manly."

"Oh, Georgia thinks he's a homosexual?"

"Yeah, that's right, one of them. Queer as a football bat."

"Why's she afraid of the sheriff?"

"Who knows," Jewel said. "Lots of colored folks are."

"How come?"

"Well, hell, Doc, I don't know. Guess 'cause he's the law. Colored folks just generally not on a first-name friends basis with the law, that's all. I guess he's no worse or no better than the rest, but I've heard some in my neighborhood say at times he can be as mean as a cornered skunk."

"Okay, Jewel, thanks for the news. I'm not sure what I'm supposed to do with it, but I think I'll just let the mean ol' sheriff handle it, and my advice to you is to do the same."

"Well, I just thought it was interestin'. Ain't you the least bit curious 'bout who this Lucky fellow is?"

"Jewel, I've got to get to the office," the doctor said as he got up from the table. "See you tonight."

"Put those dishes in the sink, Doc."

But the doctor was already out the door. As he drove to his office, he thought about what Jewel had told him, and he did have to admit to himself that he was curious about this man Lucky and how he might have been associated with Martin and the man's death. But he didn't quite know what to do about it—that is until he arrived at his office and Nadyne, as punctual and organized as ever, laid out his schedule for the day with him.

"You've got the Jackson girl at nine," she informed him. "Then Mrs. Murphy. Curtis next. And then Lawrence Johnson about his rheumatism, as usual. I'm sure something else will pop up, but that's all that's scheduled so far for this morning. This afternoon, you got house calls at Jim Ferguson's place to check on his father, Big Charley, then to Martha Madison's, who did something to her ankle, and you need to make your weekly rounds at the Wesley Home. And while you're out there, could you drop by the San Blas Lighthouse? That poor Mrs. Martin just now called and said her son had a bad sore throat, and I said you could probably drop by this afternoon, since you'd be out that way anyway, and save her a trip in, especially after all she's been through lately, bless her heart."

"Of course. Why don't you call her and let her know that I'll be there between four and five. And, by the way, did you report Liz Wright's beating to Chief Lane?"

"I did, but, as I suspected, he didn't seem too interested. I'd bet the chances of him doing anything about it are pretty slim."

"Okay, thanks Nadyne. Got any other ideas?

"No, not really, but I'll keep my eyes and ears opened. You know small towns. Hard to keep a secret like that for long."

The doctor couldn't wait to see Sally Martin again. Not only would he get to be in her presence, but he could also ask her about this Lucky fellow and maybe even stop by the nearby Indian Pass Raw Bar that kept cropping up. He had driven past it innumerable times, but had never actually gone in it. He figured now was as good a time as any.

"And, Nadyne, could you give Jewel a call and tell her that I won't be home for supper tonight. I'll be dining at the Indian Pass Raw Bar."

"Doc, you sure you want to eat out there?" Nadyne asked. "It doesn't have the best reputation in the world, in case you don't know."

"So I've heard. But I intend to find out for myself."

The day took forever. Traffic around town was heavier than it used to be with more and more people moving in to work in the new mill. It now took him longer than expected to get almost everywhere, but he kept himself occupied, from one patient to the next, with the thought of Sally Martin. She was so beautiful and unaffected. He had never been with a redhead before and, for some odd reason, this fascinated him too. He couldn't really put a finger on it, but he was surely attracted to her.

But first he had to endure his weekly visit to the Wesley Home, a Methodist-sponsored warehouse for the old, decrepit, and discarded. He knew that if he were ever faced with such a fate, he would accelerate his plans for a quick, painless way to call it quits once and for all. Anything, he thought, would be better than being left there to die like its thirty or so sorry residents, stuffed, like old socks, into the dark corner of this body bin—worn, torn, and long forgotten. Maybe an overdose of morphine or cyanide—he'd definitely concoct something that would be fast and final. He entered each room with trepidation, because the prognosis for each was always the same, one diseased way or another—they were all dying and it was now just a matter of time, for some a few scant years, for others a month or so, or even less, before their breathing stopped and Julian Fleming's discreetly plain, black panel van pulled up and hauled them away forever. At least they wouldn't have to bear the God-awful, rotting smell of the place and the sight of death constantly staring them in the face, as the doctor now had to withstand as he made his grim rounds one more time. At least this time he had something to look forward to when he was finished.

The doctor again pondered his unusual repugnance for what he understood all too well to be everyone's ultimate fate. It was not only the mounting realization of his own looming demise, but also the slow death of his second wife, Carrie Jo, from breast cancer, that made the prospect so repellent. Carrie Jo had been so good to him after Annie had disappeared, nursing him patiently back to some semblance of normality and keeping his practice going long after he had lost interest in it. Then, when he had diagnosed her with cancer, he had to slowly, helplessly watch her fade away. It had been one of the lowest points in his life to see her die and did much more to fortify his atheistic feelings than any deep religious or philosophical thinking on his part. Carrie Jo's death had, in fact, hardened the doctor's approach to life in general, more than any other event since Annie's disappearance, and the lingering memory of it still made it difficult for him to enjoy as much as he should the few pleasing parts of what was left of his own waning existence.

Finally he was on Highway 30 heading south out of Port St. Joe, then off to the right on Florida Route 30A, down the coast for a few miles until he came to the right turnoff to Cape San Blas. Despite the town's cursed past, its primary, overriding lure lay in its natural beauty. The sea seemed to be everywhere, particularly on the narrow cape where the water bordered the white sand dunes so closely on both sides that you could almost reach out and touch it with both hands. Someday a hurricane would come and flood the thin, barrier peninsula, turning it into an island or a shallow reef. Or perhaps it would just erode away gradually. It was just a matter of time. A pine and palmetto jungle, teaming with wildlife, still flanked the road from the town to the cape, despite the best efforts of the lumber mills to decimate it all. The doctor had grown to love all this, in spite of the town's seemingly endless problems, and he figured it was as good a place as any to live out his remaining days and die.

If he were to continue left a mile or so on Route 30A, he would arrive at the infamous Indian Pass Raw Bar. But that would come later. Now he was driving, car windows open to the warm spring breeze, to see Sally Martin, and, despite his persistent thoughts of death and sad memories of Carrie Jo, he found himself whistling some long-forgotten tune for the first time in a very long time.

Chapter Ten

When the doctor arrived at the lighthouse, he found Harvey Winn where he had left him one week before, sitting on his front porch in a rocking chair, smoking a pipe. This time the man held a long-handled hoe in his lap and was sharpening it with a rusty file. The doctor slowed to a stop in front of the keeper's house.

"How's it going, Mr. Winn?" the doctor hollered out the car window.

"Can't complain. How about y'all? To what do we owe the pleasure?"

"One of the Martin boys has a sore throat. Gonna see what I can do for him."

"So I hear. Hope it ain't nothing serious. You know I think the world of Sally and her kids. I don't know what me and my family would have done without them all these years. It'd be awfully lonely out here without them."

"How many children do you have?" the doctor inquired.

"Five altogether, and most of them just around the same age as the Martin's, except for Preston. He's eighteen now and off in a CCC camp down in Highlands County, near Sebring."

"So y'all must be pretty close way out here all by yourselves?"

"Yes," the lighthouse keeper said, "I'd say so. Maybe too close at times, but, as I said, we wouldn't have survived without 'em. Now, I don't know what's gonna happen. I guess the Martins will be leavin' sometime, and I'm not too happy about stickin' around without them. We'll see. Hope Ronald's okay."

"Me too. I better go ahead and check on him now. Good to see you again, Mr. Winn," the doctor said and drove on a few more yards to the Martin house.

Sally Martin greeted the doctor at the cottage's front door. She was no longer in black, but instead in a crisp, white, sleeveless shift that hinted shyly of her slim figure. She smiled as she opened the screen door.

"Good to see you again, Doctor," she said. "Thanks for coming all the way out here. It's probably nothing serious, but the boy does seem to be in some pain. I'll get him for you."

"It's no problem at all, Mrs. Martin. I had to be out at the Wesley Home today anyway."

"Sally," she said. "Why don't you call me Sally. Mrs. sounds so formal."

"Okay, Sally, but only if you'll call me Van. Hardly anyone does anymore, and I sort of miss the sound of it."

"Okay, if you say so, Doctor—I mean, Van. I'll be right back."

He watched her hips as she ascended the narrow stairs and soon returned with a cute, blond-headed little boy who said his name was Ronald.

"How old are you, Ronald?" the doctor asked.

"Six."

"Can you swallow and breathe okay?"

"Yes, sir."

"Does this hurt?" the doctor asked as he pressed the lymph nodes in the boy's neck. "No? Okay, good. Can you open wide for me and say 'ah' when I put this stick on your tongue."

"Aaaah."

"Good. Now I'm going to put this thermometer under your tongue, and I want you to close your mouth and don't open it until I tell you to, okay?"

"Yes, sir."

"His throat is inflamed all right," the doctor told the boy's mother. "But his tonsils look okay. Has he been eating all right?"

"Yes, he had breakfast and dinner and ate everything."

"Good, his temperature is normal," the doctor said, holding the thermometer up to the light.

"I'd say he's probably suffering from all this pollen in the air this time of year. Kids his age are often susceptible. Does he have any allergies?"

"No, not really. He gets stuffy sometimes, but nothing serious."

"I don't suspect the boy knows how to gargle yet, so see if you can get a cup of apple cider vinegar tea down him three or four times a day until he stops hurting. Have you prepared it before?"

"No."

"Just heat up a cup of water, add a teaspoon of apple cider vinegar, a teaspoon of honey, and a squeeze or two of lemon juice. Some people put in a pinch of cayenne pepper, but I'd leave that out for a child his age. If he doesn't get better in a couple of days, give me a call. And then the next time I'm out this way, I'll stop by to make sure the inflammation is gone."

"Okay, thank you so much, Doctor."

"Van," the doctor corrected.

"Oh, yes, of course, Van. Well, Van, I hate to say this after dragging you all the way out here, but until we get Earl's life insurance straightened out, I really can't afford to pay you. But, if you don't have other plans, we'd love to have you stay for supper. Maybe that would at least make your trip out here worthwhile."

Any thoughts the doctor had of eating that evening at the Indian Pass Raw Bar were immediately dashed. "Of course, I'd be delighted," he told her.

"Well then, good. You have your choice. You can sit out on the front porch and enjoy the sea breeze or you can keep me company in the kitchen while the kids and I finish getting supper ready."

"I'd prefer your company, if you don't mind."

"Good, follow me."

He did follow her, his eyes again glued to her slim hips, as she led him inside. While the doctor sat at the kitchen table and sipped the iced tea that she had put before him, he watched Sally Martin confidently coordinate her family in putting together their supper. Earlene, the eldest at thirteen, who the doctor had seen two days ago at City Hall, was instructed to go to the garden and cut some asparagus spears. John, her younger brother by a year, was told to start a fire in the backyard fireplace. And Roseanne, the little girl who had discovered her dead father just last week, and her ailing younger brother, Ronald, were given the task of setting the table.

"And all of you, wash your hands good with soap and water before you do anything," their mother instructed.

"Okay, how's this sound?" she asked him as the children crowded around the kitchen sink. "I'll put these new potatoes on to boil now. Ever had salt potatoes?"

"No, I don't believe I have," the doctor said.

"Old Irish family recipe. Just dump a bunch of new potatoes, like these that I dug up this morning in the garden, into a pot of boiling salt water. Trick is to use a lot of salt. That's it. Some recipe, huh? But just you wait and see, the only way you'll eat new potatoes again. Then I have a pan full of whole, cleaned bluefish in some milk in the icebox—the milk cuts the oiliness. A school of bluefish came in today and the boys and Harvey have been pulling them out one after another since they got home from school. Ever seen a big school of bluefish come in almost to shore?"

"No, I don't believe I have."

"It's like a cauldron. Fish jumping like popcorn everywhere. It's a sight! Tomorrow, Mary Winn and I'll start smoking the ones we don't eat tonight. Harvey's built us a little smokehouse out back, and we'll get a good driftwood fire going and hang those fish up over it for a few hours. We'll be eating them till they're comin' out our ears. But now, when the fire out back burns down in a few minutes, John will take the fish out of the milk and grill them while Earlene steams the asparagus which we're gonna top with a big hunk of butter. And for dessert I baked that rhubarb pie that's cooling over there on the windowsill. The rhubarb is fresh from the garden too. Sound good?"

"Sounds more than good. Call me out here and don't pay my any time you like," the doctor said.

Everything was prepared just as Sally had described, and everything was more delicious than he could have imagined. The table was surprisingly quiet for six people. The children were shy and exceedingly polite, apprehensive, he thought, at just meeting him and having him there at their kitchen table instead of their father. Sally asked them about their day at school, and the children mumbled courteous, but curt answers and continued eating until every scrap of the meal they had prepared was gone. The doctor was quiet too. He hadn't sat down for supper with an entire family with kids, except for Jewel and Marcus, since he was a child himself, so he didn't know quite what to do. But, despite their awkwardness, he did find himself enjoying himself and savoring both the food and the constrained company.

"I insist now," Sally said, when everyone was finished eating, "that you go out on the porch and relax. I'll put the children to cleaning up and join you in a few minutes."

The doctor thanked the children for preparing such an outstanding meal and went out on the front porch, as instructed. It was another beautiful night and he thought about how sad it was that this serene, solitary place had to be marred by such misfortune and morbidity. It was a tribute to man's resilience, he thought, that someone as delicate as Sally Martin could withstand it all and still remain as sweet and appealing as she was to the doctor. He wondered what stood in store for both of them as he watched the sun blaze brilliantly across the cloudless sky on its way into the wide horizon of the Gulf of Mexico.

Chapter Eleven

Sally Martin soon joined the doctor on the front porch and sat down in the rocking chair next to him. Without a word, they watched the day turning into night. And just as the orange ball of sun disappeared below the horizon, there suddenly shot straight upwards into the sky and across the horizon a bright, narrow green ray, like the quick flash of a lighthouse beam.

"Did you see that?" the doctor asked.

"Yes, what was it?"

"The green ray," he said. "Very rare and very beautiful."

"Yes, it was beautiful. I've never seen it before. What causes it?"

"No one is sure," the doctor answered. "Some guess that it's the last bit of sunlight shining through the spray of the ocean's whitecaps. Jules Verne wrote a novel about it a few years back called *Le Rayon-Vert.* He claimed that there was an ancient legend surrounding it, and, according to the legend, those who are fortunate enough to see the green ray are incapable of being deceived in matters of sentiment. They are able to see closely into their own hearts and to read the thoughts of others."

"Do you believe that?" she asked.

"Well, I guess we shall see," the doctor said.

As the sky slowly darkened, they sat in silence, listening to the waves break across the sand, watching brown pelicans skim just above the sea's surface searching for supper.

"You have wonderful children," the doctor said finally.

"Thank you. I do marvel sometimes at how they are growing up and even maturing, the older two, anyway. It's been hard for them, I think, living out here where it's so quiet and isolated. Thank goodness for the Winn children next door or they would have never survived. How about you? Do you have children?"

"No," the doctor said. "I'm sorry to say that I've never been blessed. God knows I've tried, but, I'm afraid, unsuccessfully. The specialists can't seem to figure out why, but, in any case, none of my three wives ever got pregnant."

"Three?"

"Yes, I hate to admit it, but, yes, three. The first, Annie, who I met in college, disappeared in nineteen twenty-seven, after we'd been married for almost thirty years. I had a hard time with that, but I'd gotten use to being married, I guess, so I married again . . . to Carrie Jo, my nurse. She died from cancer after we'd been married for only about four years. And then Jennie—she divorced me about three years ago after we'd been married only a little more than a year."

"What happened? If you don't mind me asking?"

"With Jennie? Well now, that's a good question. I wish I knew exactly. The truth is I was always in love with Annie, my first wife, and when she disappeared, I think I tried to replace her with Carrie Jo and then Jennie, but, of course, that didn't work. Neither Carrie Jo nor Jennie wanted to be replacements. The simple fact is that I wasn't much of a husband after I lost Annie. Carrie Jo was sweet to put up with me, but Jennie couldn't, wouldn't, didn't have the patience."

"The divorce," she murmured, "was it hard?"

"Yes, of course, but not that unexpected. Jennie was not a happy woman before or after me. I thought I could make her happy, but I was wrong. I couldn't."

"I thought I could make Earl happy too. Maybe I did for a while. But, in the end, he was not a happy man." She paused for a moment and then said, "I told him that I wanted a divorce."

"Because of the drinking and gambling?" the doctor asked.

"Yes, partly, but more because of his absence. He just wasn't around much, physically, emotionally, anyway. We really weren't much of a couple anymore. Maybe we could have made it if he hadn't put us so much in debt, but he was draining us. It got to the point that we would all be better off without him. And now I feel terrible that I told him that. I have to believe this whole thing is my fault."

"In what way?"

"In January I told Earl I wanted a divorce. It was my secret New Year's resolution—to get away from Earl. Then I find out from this insurance fellow that a few days after I told Earl that he upped the value of his policy. That must have been the big plan that he said he had—to up the insurance policy and then get himself killed so we could get out of debt and get on with our lives without him, after I told him we would be better off without him."

"But he clearly didn't kill himself. And, anyway, he had to know about the suicide exclusion in the insurance policy. And didn't his uncle arrange a loan, so wouldn't that have solved the money problem?"

"Well, the insurance man who came out here on Wednesday after the meeting seems to think that Earl may have hired someone to kill him so we would get the money."

"I know. He told me the same thing. But, as I asked the insurance man, why would Earl do that if he was going to get a loan?"

"I don't know. This loan arrangement just came up last week, a few days before Earl was attacked. It hadn't been finalized with the bank yet—probably never will be now, I guess. Earl's uncle was handling it all."

"Did you tell all this to the insurance man?"

"No," she said. "I didn't say anything about Earl and me having trouble, or a divorce, or a plan, or anything like that. There was just something about the man. I had the feeling that he was not entirely on my side."

"I think your feeling was probably right. His job is to be suspicious, and he seems to take his job pretty seriously. He's definitely on the insurance company's side and not necessarily yours."

"Well, I really don't know who to turn to at this point. We surely do need the insurance money to hold us until I can get a job. The insurance man said he needed to complete his investigation before we get anything, but he didn't tell me how long that would take. I wish I could sort this all through. I wish I knew what Earl was up to and who killed him. And I just wish this was all over." She began to cry again, softly this time so that the doctor could barely hear her.

"Let me see what I can do," he said. "I'm gonna go by the Indian Pass Raw Bar tonight. It keeps popping up. Seems that Earl spent quite a bit of time out there. Did he mention any names of people he knew there?"

"No, not that I recall. For a man who spent as much time as he did out there, he sure didn't say much about it."

"Anything at all that might help me find out about all this?"

"No," she said. "I can't think of anything. I know he went out there about every night, and I know he came home late, just before he had to tend the light, smelling like a brewery and with a lot less money than he left with. And that's about all I know."

Just then a child's cry came from upstairs and Sally said, "Oh no, I forgot to give Ronald his apple cider vinegar tea. I better go do that."

"Do you remember the recipe?

"Ugh, yes, I'm afraid I do. I hope he'll drink it. I know I won't."

"Add a little extra honey. You'll both love it," he said in his most reassuring doctor voice.

"Okay, we'll see. I better go tend to him now."

"All right," he said, as they both stood up, "I'll see if I can find out anything that will help us make sense of all this. And thank you so much for supper. It was truly delicious."

He put his hand on her bare arm and then lightly kissed her cheek. She turned her head just as he did so and their lips met—accidentally, he was not sure?—but he did not move until, in an ever-so-brief moment, she pulled away, blushing, and hurried back inside the house.

"Be careful," she said through the screen door.

"Goodnight."

By now it was dark and the doctor was tired, but he decided, now that he had told Sally he would, to go the Indian Pass Raw Bar to see what, if anything, he could find out that would help them understand what happened to poor Earl Martin. The full moon was now large and bright in the cloudless sky, paving, along with the sharp flash from the light tower above, a glimmering path across the silent sea.

Chapter Twelve

The Indian Pass Raw Bar was located at the corner of Route 30A and Indian Pass Road, about five miles due east of the Cape San Blas Lighthouse, in a weathered, white clapboard building surrounded by a crushed seashell parking lot and a thick longleaf pine forest. The unlit lot was filled with cars and trucks when the doctor pulled in and finally found a narrow spot at the rear of the building. There were several high piles of empty oyster shells lining the back of the building, and hanging on rusty hooks on the wall were about a dozen sharp-pronged oyster rakes—similar to pitch forks, but with longer handles and several wickedly curved steel tines.

Inside, the doctor found a large, dimly lit room filled with round, wooden tables and chairs, a Wurlitzer jukebox in the corner blaring Roy Acuff's "Wabash Cannon Ball," and a long, crowded cypress bar extending the length of one wall to the left of the front door. The place smelled of tobacco smoke, sweat, and stale beer and was filled with working men, fishermen, farmers, and turpentiners, all still in their worn work clothes clamoring to spend their weekly pay on beer, barbecue, and raw oysters.

The doctor suddenly realized how out of place he looked in his suit and tie, but it was too late to do anything about that now.

The roadhouse was so dark and smoky that he could barely see from one end of it to the other. He thought he could make out a few vaguely familiar faces, men he had treated sometime in the past for some forgotten ailments, but there was not one that he could actually put a name to. He found an empty stool at the far end of the bar and ordered a Spearman beer from the busy bartender. So this was where Earl Martin spent his free time. The doctor frankly did not see the attraction. He would have much rather been back on Cape San Blas with the man's wife. And how in the world was he supposed to find anything out about Martin or Lucky or whoever might know anything about them? After a second beer, an old, bald-headed man in bib overalls and blue work shirt sat down on the stool next to him and the doctor offered to buy him a drink.

"Pabst," he told the bartender. "What brings you out here? Don't believe I've seen you before."

"No, this is my first time," the doctor told him. "Driven past often enough. Just thought I'd drop in and see what's going on. And I'm looking for someone."

"Who's that?"

"Fellow named Lucky. I owe him some money and I was told I might be able to find him here," the doctor blurted, having just come up with the story.

"Never heard of him. You some kind of cop or something? There was another guy in here the other night looking around for friends of that man who got killed out at the lighthouse."

"No, I'm no cop, just a business man."

"Well, sorry I can't help you. You might try the owner, Sadie. She's the one over there at the cash register. She pretty much knows everything 'bout everybody around here."

The doctor thanked the man and shook his hand. He knew he had been brushed off as some kind of nosy interloper, and he suddenly had to wonder at his own stupid naivety for coming here. He was not good at this at all. Nevertheless, the doctor pushed on, excusing himself to find the gray-haired owner/cashier who was sitting near the front door behind an ancient cash register that looked about as old as she did.

"Do you mind if I join you for a minute?" he asked her, as Bob Wills and The Texas Playboys launched into "Steel Guitar Rag" on the jukebox.

"Suit yourself," she answered, as she counted a stack of wrinkled one dollar bills, slowly and methodically one by one, "but I'm sort of busy here, as you can see."

Actually, aside from the counting job, she didn't look that busy at all. True, the place was packed, but no one seemed to be too eager to stop eating and drinking just yet and take their bill to pay her. Instead, it looked like the kind of place where men were likely to continue drinking well into the night.

The doctor found an empty chair and dragged it up next to hers. "Always this busy?" he asked.

"Heavens, no. I wish it was. It's 'cause it's Friday night. Pay day. Nice night. Full moon. Everybody's out. What brings you out?"

The doctor decided to take a different tack this time. When all else fails, he thought, try honesty. "My name's Van Berber," he said. "I'm a doctor in Port St. Joe. I sort of got involved in this Martin death at the lighthouse and was wondering if you might be able to help me?"

"Well, Doctor, I'll do what I can, but let me tell you somethin', the same thing I told that insurance man and the sheriff when he was in here yesterday. I've been running this place for thirty-five years now. Started out in nineteen-oh-three as a commissary for the turpentine camp that was out back. Did so good we built this place in twenty-nine when they put in the new highway out front. Now, I don't make a lot of money off it, but I do make a livin', and the two things I've learnt all them years is: number one, you offer up a fair plate for a fair price, chances are people'll come back, and second, you pass on a secret that someone tells in here, they'll never come back. So I don't tell no secrets. I keep my mouth shut."

"Well, I can appreciate that," the doctor said. "I wouldn't expect you tell any secrets. I was just wondering if you knew this Martin fellow and who his friends were."

"I did know him, since he came in here 'most every night, and I guess that ain't no secret. Anybody'll tell you that. As far as his friends went, I'd consider that a secret, wouldn't you?"

"What kind of a guy was he, Mr. Martin?"

"He was a customer. A good customer. Sometimes got behind on his bill, but that's my fault. Shouldn't have let him run it."

"Anything else?"

"No, not really."

"Was he a gambler?" the doctor asked.

"Couldn't tell you."

"Know a fellow named Lucky?"

"Was a man named Lucky come in here, but ain't seen him for over a week now."

"Do you remember when you last saw him?"

"No, can't recall. Like I said, 'bout a week ago."

"Can you tell me what he looked like."

"Tall man, curly-haired, dark, Eye-talian, I believe."

"Was he a friend of Martin's?"

"Couldn't say."

"Anything else you could tell me that might help the man's family?"

"No, Doctor, I wish I could, but that's about it."

"You sure?" the doctor said.

"Yes," the old lady answered, looking him directly in the eye, "'Cept my advice to you and the man's family would be to stay as far away as possible from this man Lucky."

"And why is that?"

"Just trust me, Doctor. Stay away. That's all I'm gonna say."

The doctor knew it was hopeless to push the woman any further and the smoke was burning his eyes, so he went outside and stood on the long covered porch that extended the width of the building's front. He rested there for a moment by himself, breathing in the cool, salty air, and listened to the crickets, the cicadas, and the tree frogs chirping emphatically in the surrounding woods. The full moon was now resting huge and bright orange against the dark horizon. And the doctor was achy and tired. He wondered what the hell he was doing here. He was no detective. Who did he think he was anyway? The insurance investigator, Stanton, and the sheriff had already been here and found out more than he had. And what was this with Sally Martin—falling for a woman at least twenty years his junior? Was he becoming demented in his old age? Or was he just a sad, old fool? No fool like an old fool, as Jewel would say. Was Sally Martin just looking for a father figure to help her through a rough time? Was he completely misreading what he read as a fondness between them? The doctor wasn't sure anymore about any of this. But he did know that it had been a long day and he was exhausted. He wanted to go home, have a nip of morphine, and go to bed. So he slowly walked back around the roadhouse through the long moon shadows to his car. The baying of the tree frogs occasionally stopped, and when they did the doctor could clearly hear his footsteps crunch on the hard, loose shells of the parking lot. As he rounded the rear corner of the building a few feet from his car, the night sounds ceased for a brief moment and he thought he heard the sounds of someone else's footsteps behind him, or was it just an echo of his own steps? He was afraid to look, so he hurried on among the parked cars to where he remembered parking his own car. Finally, as the shadows of the high pines darkened his path, he found the old Ford right where he had left it. He dug into his pocket for his keys and finally found them. Just as he was about to open the car's door a quickly moving shadow suddenly descended upon him from behind. And, as he was about to turn, he felt an immense force and the most excruciating pain that he had ever felt ripping fiercely into his shoulders. He heard someone shout "stop!"—was it him? Running. He felt himself falling fast toward the car, too fast to stop, and then everything was black.

Chapter Thirteen

The doctor was not sure, but he thought he heard a light tapping at the glass window pane in his front door. He hauled himself up from his worn leather chair where he was reading the Port St. Joe *Star* and went to the door. There, miraculously, after all these years, stood his first wife, pretty Annie, in her white spring dress, as stunning and radiant as ever.

"Darling," he said. "Where have you been?"

"On a trip, of course, on a very long trip. Aren't you going to invite me in?"

"Yes, of course, come in, come in," he said excitedly, taking the two leather suitcases from her, the ones he had bought her for her fortieth birthday with the gold-embossed monograms: AEB. He couldn't believe that she had finally returned.

"Come, let's celebrate," he said, taking a dusty bottle of muscadine wine from the cupboard shelf.

"How have you been?" she asked, sitting primly in his parlor with her tiny hands clasped on her lap.

"Okay, I guess, but I've missed you terribly. How about you? It's been so long. I've so much to tell you."

"Yes, I can't wait," she said, taking a sip of her wine. "I have much to tell you too. Are you going to tell me that you've found someone else?"

"No, Annie, I've been waiting for you. No one could ever replace you."

"Are you sure? I've been having the strangest feeling lately that you've found someone new, a striking redhead, if I'm not mistaken."

"No, no," he protested.

"Are you sure? I know how easily you fall in love, Van."

"No, no, no!"

"Doctor, it's okay. You're dreaming," said a familiar voice, not Annie's. He opened his eyes and there was his nurse, Nadyne, looking concerned over her glasses and holding his hand.

"Nadyne, where am I?"

"In your office, Doctor. In the emergency room of your office."

The doctor found himself lying shirtless and face down on the operating table, and he craned his head up to see Nadyne, Gator Mica, and Sheriff Batson surrounding him in the little room. "What happened?" he asked.

"You got whacked pretty good by an oyster rake, partner," Gator reported, looking ill at ease in the cramped white room with its bright lights making everyone look a little spooky, he thought.

"A what?" the doctor asked.

"Yeah, sure 'nough, an oyster rake, what they use to rake oysters off the bottom of the bay with. Some guy was about to poke you full of holes like a sieve until I came along and run him off."

"What were you doing there?" the doctor asked, still confused by the entire situation.

"I went by your house to get you earlier this evening. There was this whole big school of bluefish moving up along the coast. Man, you ought to have seen 'em, bubblin' up like boilin' water. We could've caught a ton. But, instead, Jewel says you're out at the Indian Pass Raw Bar, God knows why. So, on my way home, I stopped by there to see if I could find you and what do I find but some guy trying to turn you into a sponge. He got one good whack in before I could stop him and you went face first into the running board of your car. I gave chase, but the man was too fast for me. Once he got into the woods, he was long gone. Besides I wanted to see if you was still alive, so I came back to get you, and you was out colder than a codfish, so I brought you into town and went and got Nadyne out of bed. She opened up the office and patched you up and called the sheriff, who just now walked in."

"Did you get a look at him?" the sheriff asked.

"No, not a good one," Gator said. "He was in between those cars and out into the woods before I had a chance to see much, but he looked sort of tall and rangy with either a hat or a head full of curly hair." Why did that sound familiar to the doctor? He couldn't remember exactly. He was drowsy, but he didn't seem to be in any pain.

"Nadyne, what's the damage? Am I going to live?"

"Yeah, I'm afraid so, Doctor. When the morphine wears off, you'll maybe wish you weren't, because you got four big holes in your back, each as deep as your shoulder blade. I cleaned them out real good with alcohol, since you were unconscious, and smeared them with mercurochrome and bandaged them up. You're just gonna hurt for a while until they heal. As far as the bump on your forehead, well, it's a good thing you have such a hard head, because I can't see any damage besides a nasty-looking bruise and a big bump."

"You need to order me some tetanus toxoid vaccine, Nadyne. It's just new on the market, but if that oyster rake was as rusty as most, I'm a good candidate for lock jaw even if you did clean me up good. You should be able to get it from our usual supplier."

"Okay, Doctor. Tetanus toxoid. Got it," Nadyne said, as she looked around for something to write it down with.

"Doctor, I know this might not be the best time to get into this," the sheriff said, "but what the hell were you doing out at the Indian Pass Raw Bar in the first place?"

"That's a real good question, Sheriff. I was asking myself the very same thing just before the lights went out. Curiosity more than anything, I guess. Everyone kept talking about it and then Mrs. Martin asked me to help, so being the chivalrous fool that I am, I decided to take a ride out there."

"Not a very wise decision," the sheriff noted. "But anyway, did you find anything out while you were there that might help us with this case, besides that whoever killed Martin looks like he's still running around loose?"

"Well, as you might imagine, Sheriff, the folks out there weren't all that open with me. Let me see, the lady who owned the place said Martin owed her some money, was apparently behind on his bill, but she didn't look like the type who would kill a man for an overdue bar bill."

"What about friends, or enemies, of Martin, anyone talk about that?"

"Well, let me see," the doctor said, racking his fussy brain for something he knew was there but that he couldn't quite pinpoint.

"Well, it looks to me like you're lucky that Gator showed up when he did," the sheriff said.

That was it: Lucky. Who was he? "Yes, Lucky, someone, the owner/cashier lady mentioned him. Said he was a friend of Martin. The old lady said he was tall, dark, curly-haired. Wait, that's the guy who tried to kill me, right?"

"Sounds like it," the sheriff said. "Anything else?"

"Yes, she said she thought he was Italian. How she knows that she didn't say."

There was a long moment of silence as if everyone was trying to absorb this new information and determine what to do next. The doctor was awfully thirsty and wondered what time it was.

"Okay, look," the sheriff finally said, "I want you to stay clear of that place. You understand? Take a few days off. Let your back heal up. I'll ask the chief to send around a patrol car as often as he can to keep an eye on you. Keep your doors locked. I've got a good enough description of this guy that I can send it to Tallahassee to see if they have anybody who's wanted who matches it. Meanwhile, I'll continue to ask around about this Lucky fellow. Somebody has to know more than we know about him now. I'm of a good mind to close that damn bar down until Sadie McIntire or someone else decides to give up some of those goddamn secrets they keep keepin' out there. The place is a menace. Something bad always goin' on out there. Right, Gator?"

"Sure, Sheriff. You ready to go home, partner?" Gator asked the doctor.

"Yeah, I am," the doctor said. "If I can just get up."

Chapter Fourteen

Nadyne had shot the doctor so full of morphine that he slept soundly until she arrived at his house the next morning to check on him. As he lay helplessly face down on his bed, she slowly, carefully removed the bandages and reported that everything looked good on his back. It was maddening for the doctor not to be able to see his own wounds, but he couldn't think of anyone who he trusted more than Nadyne to tend to them. She, as always, was gentle, meticulous, and frank, and, if he had to be broken, at least he had Nadyne to fix him.

"Since it's the weekend, Doctor, you don't have any appointments," she said. "If someone calls here with an emergency, tell them to call me at home or go to the Panama City Hospital. I'll cover your appointments next week or until you're feeling better. Don't worry about a thing. Jewel's going to look in on you too. So all you need to do is holler, if you need anything. Want me to shoot you up with morphine again?"

"No," the doctor said. "It makes me too woozy. I've got some here if I need it. Just stay for a few more minutes while I take a shower. Then you can bandage me up again.

"Okay, Doctor. I'll make some coffee while you're in the shower."

He had not taken any more morphine yet this morning and his back ached, but he wanted to feel the pain for a little while as a way of gauging just how bad off he really was. The sting was intense when the hot water hit his back, and he had to be careful drying off, but he thought just a little more than his usual morning dose should see him through as long as no one decided to slap him on the back.

Soon after Nadyne had applied new bandages and left, the doctor heard Jewel downstairs in the kitchen making breakfast. It took him awhile, but he finally finished dressing and gingerly made his way down the stairs and to the kitchen table. Ordinarily, the doctor was left to his own devices on Saturday and Sunday, while Jewel was at home with Marcus and her mother. There were always plenty of leftovers in the icebox, and he just let the dirty dishes pile up for Jewel to deal with when she returned Monday morning.

"Mornin,' Doc," Jewel greeted him. "I want you to know you missed your one and only chance of havin' breakfast in bed. I was fixin' to bring it up to you, but here you are. How you doin'? You look like you was sent fo' and couldn't come."

"Well, I've been better. I think my pride is hurt more than my back, if you want to know the truth. My big chance at being a hot-shot detective and I end up out cold. Oh, well."

"Did you find out anything?" she inquired as she set a cup of black coffee and a plate of ham and eggs in front of him.

"No, not much," he said and then filled her in on everything he knew about Lucky and the Indian Pass Raw Bar.

"I'll check it out, Doc. Someone has to know more about this man."

"Jewel, I'm thinking, after last night, that maybe we should just butt out and let the sheriff handle this thing. That's what we pay him to do after all."

"Well, it won't hurt to nose around a little. Don't you want to know what the samhill's goin' on here? If I find out anything, we'll give it to the sheriff and let him chase this guy down."

"I'm not going to argue with you, Jewel. I know by now that it won't do any good anyway. So what's new with you? I hope I'm not ruining your weekend."

"No, just the usual. I got a blue million things to do today. Catchin' up on some mendin', and Marcus needs some new pants. Boy's growin' like a weed, outgrown everything. So we're goin' shopping. I need a new dress. Gabriel's comin' to town in a few days, so I need to look pretty. He's going to sing over at Ziglers in Apalachicola and here over at the Ebony Club for a few nights. Should be a fun time."

"Sounds like it. You're bringing him by here, aren't you? I need to get brought up to date on the latest blues music, and I know they won't let me in at the Ebony Club."

"Sure," she said. "You know Gabriel. Give him a drink and somethin' to eat and the man'll sing all night. But, Doc, you know you welcome at the Ebony Club any time you want. Just 'cause you white don't mean nothin'. Makes no never mind to us colored folks. It's you white folks don't like us colored people in your places, not the other way around."

"Well, I know how I felt at the Indian Pass Raw Bar last night as the only person in the place with a suit and tie on, so I can only imagine how I'd stand out at the Ebony Club. Maybe someday."

"You're always welcome, Doc."

"Thanks, Jewel, I appreciate that. Now could you get me another cup of coffee and then get the hell out of here? I'm going to milk this injury as an excuse to listen to the radio and catch up on some reading without anybody bothering me or feeling guilty."

"Okay, Doc, I'll check on you tomorrow after church. There's plenty of leftovers in the icebox. Meantime, call me if you need anything."

"Thanks, Jewel, goodbye."

"Oh, one more thing," she said as she was going out the back door. "Put those dishes in the sink for me, will you?"

The doctor did not answer her. Instead, he finished his breakfast and hobbled back upstairs to the bathroom to look in the mirror. He didn't like the way Nadyne and Jewel had been looking at him, like he was dying or something. He did look a little pale, unshaven too, with a nasty-looking blue bump on his forehead. He had dark circles under his blue eyes, and his black hair was thinning and turning gray around the edges. When did all this happen? He *was* dying, or at least turning into an old man, there was no doubt about that. He looked down at his stomach. He had a definite paunch, not real pronounced, but no longer flat either. His legs were still skinny, but his skin everywhere had an undeniable pallid look. He needed to get outside more and get more exercise. Maybe he would look better after his head and back healed. Maybe he should start paying more attention to how he looked. Maybe next week.

He couldn't lie on his back, and he couldn't comfortably lie on his stomach and read, so he turned on the radio and listened in disgust as he heard the announcer report on the events in Austria. A couple of weeks before, Adolf Hitler and his Nazi troops had marched into Austria and taken over the country unopposed, quickly expelling all Jews and other political opponents from the universities. Now, Herman Goering, Hitler's henchman, was warning *all* Jews to leave the country. The doctor didn't know where all this was leading, but it scared the hell out of him to think of what might come next.

He was all too aware of the dangers, having heard from his father, Haig Der Berberian, about the persecution of the Armenians in the Ottoman Empire, from which he, his wife Ani, and his six-year-old son Van had fled to America in 1879. His father had told him many stories about the Bloody Sultan who had killed his grandfather, as well as two of his uncles as a part of the state-sponsored massacres that ultimately claimed the lives of nearly 300,000 Armenians in 1894. According to the doctor's father, their few remaining relatives who survived these massacres or did not leave the country were wiped out in the Armenian Genocide of 1915–1916.

He tried to sit up in a wicker chair on the screened-in back porch and read a novel called *Of Mice and Men* by this new young author named Steinbeck, but by midafternoon his back was hurting too much, so he took an extra dose of morphine and went back to bed.

Despite the morphine, he slept fitfully, and sometime in the middle of the night he awoke, drenched in sweat, from an embarrassing, lurid dream about Sally Martin. In the dream, he and Sally were lying in bed together, naked, tangled in a serpentine snarl of white, cotton sheets. Her face was buried in a pillow, and his right hand was entangled in the thick, corkscrew curls of her red hair, while the other was wrapped around her slender waist. In the dark, she turned her head and they were kissing—so passionately that the doctor couldn't catch his breath. It was as if he were being swallowed.

He gasped as he awoke, the night air, cool, strangely quiet, and heavy with dew. He rolled over and finally calmed himself, except then there was the awful pain again, shooting suddenly across his back and down through his body.

When at last he found a tolerably comfortable position, he tried to figure out what was going on with him. And who this shy, mysterious woman was who was provoking these strange, prurient dreams of an adolescent boy.

Here in the silence of the night, he felt at once too old and too weary for it all. He tried to go back to sleep, but he only found himself going back—back to another time and season—to Annie, to Carrie Jo, to Jennie—to those soothing summer nights long ago, when all that seemed to matter was their warmth and simple tenderness.

It was dawn before he realized just how lonely he had become.

Since he knew sleep would not return any time soon, he got up, gave himself a sponge bath, made coffee, and read the weekly edition of the Port St. Joe *Star* and the Sunday Panama City *News Herald.* He thought some more about the Martin murder and Sally Martin, but between the pain in his back and the haze of the morphine he couldn't focus enough to draw any conclusions or even to figure out what conclusions needed to be drawn.

He was glad to see Jewel and Marcus, in their Sunday best, arrive that afternoon with a big picnic basket that Marcus plopped unceremoniously on the kitchen counter. The doctor was still trying to read, but he couldn't seem to concentrate, so it was a welcome surprise to see Jewel looking so pretty and pleasant as usual.

"How you doin', Doc?" Jewel asked, starting to unpack the contents of the basket. "Look what the church ladies put together for you. You one lucky man. Don't know that you deserve it, but them old ladies, Doc, I swear, they all got a soft spot for you. God knows why."

"'Cause I treat 'em for free, that's why."

"Oh, ain't we sassy this afternoon. You must be feeling better. If you ain't, you sure will after this meal. Marcus, get that table set and pour the doctor a glass of sweet tea before he expires. You still lookin' a little peaked, doc. Sit down," Jewel ordered, "'fore you fall down."

They were about ready to start eating when they heard a noisy vehicle with squeaky brakes slide to a stop in the back driveway. Before they knew it, Gator Mica was upon them, rubbing Marcus's hair and squeezing Jewel around the waist, bigger than life, and, as usual, bearing gifts. He deposited his burlap bag on the kitchen counter and started unloading.

"Tomatoes, first of the year," he announced, placing them gently on the table before him. "Green onions, just pulled. Radishes, just for you, Marcus, put hair on your chest. And blackberries for the sweetest, little black berry I know. Jewel, I swear, I'll marry you if you turn 'em into cobbler. And, oh yes, for the poor invalid doctor, something that'll sure kill the pain, a nice quart of your favorite moonshine, for medicinal purposes only, of course."

"Well, tie me to a pig and roll me in mud. You're always full of surprises. Sit down, you silly man," Jewel instructed. "We'll just add it to the bounty. Looky here what the church ladies done fixed for the ungrateful doctor. Fried chicken—Marge Hinsky's—I swear I don't know how she gets it so crispy. Still warm. Tater salad—Jody Harris's—she puts somethin' in there that's addictin'. And forget your cobbler, Gator, this here's mama's own cherry pie. That's right; this here's *my* mama's—nothing better. We be havin' us some kind of picnic now. It's gonna be so good, it'll make you wanna slap yo' *own* mama."

After stuffing himself, the doctor wanted to take a nap, but Gator insisted that they all had to have a sip of moonshine on the back porch first, while Marcus, as usual, cleaned up.

"Okay, boys," Jewel said when they were all seated. "Now that I ate so much I feel like a tick about to pop, get this. I talked to Cecil Burnett after church this morning. Well, he's about as country as cornflakes, but he's still the janitor/gofer out at the Indian Pass Raw Bar. He knows this Lucky guy everybody talkin' about. Seems that he works for some guy name of Price who's a moonshiner. Accordin' to Cecil, Lucky sells Price's moonshine out of a panel truck at the back of the Indian Pass Raw Bar. Lucky pays the owner, some old lady named Sadie, to park in her lot and if anybody wants anything stronger than the beer and wine they got a license to serve at the Raw Bar, they go out back there and buy it from this fellow Lucky."

"How about Martin?" the doctor asked. "Were this Lucky and Martin buddies?"

"Yeah, accordin' to Cecil, Martin was a real drinker, and he got his booze from Lucky."

"Did Martin run a tab with this guy?" Gator asked.

"Cecil said he didn't know much more than that. This Lucky was real sort of secretive. Didn't tell anybody his full name or where he lived or much of anything more than what it cost for a jug of moonshine."

"What about this moonshiner named Price?" the doctor asked. "Maybe he knows where to find Lucky."

"I know him," Gator said matter-of-factly.

"You do? How in the world? . . . "

"He owns St. Vincent Island right across Indian Pass from me. He's got a whole, big complex over there with houses and a swimming pool and three caretaker families living there year-round. He's brought in these big ol' Sambar deer from India, and he makes some of the best moonshine in north Florida."

"But how do you know him?" the doctor asked.

"I like to oyster harvest around his island—Bay Bayou, Big Bayou, Indian Lagoon. The best oysters around here, but I knew if I got too close to his island, him being a moonshiner and all, that I might find myself headfirst in the mud at the bottom of St. Joseph Bay. And come to find out some poachers sometimes get tempted by those big deer and all the other wildlife out there, not to mention nosy revenuers, and my camp at Indian Pass just so happens to have a perfect view of the shortest channel between the mainland and St. Vincent. So me and Price made a deal. I'd keep an eye out for poachers and revenuers and run 'em off when I seen 'em, and Price would let me have as many oysters and as much moonshine as I wanted as long as I didn't sell none of it. Been workin' out pretty well for the past couple of years now."

"Fascinating," the doctor said. "Anything else you two know about that you want to share?"

"What else you wanna know, Doc?" Jewel asked.

Chapter Fifteen

It didn't take more than another day at home, what with Jewel annoyingly puttering around downstairs and his inability to lie comfortably on his back and read, before the doctor decided it was time to go back to work. So on Tuesday morning, he returned to his office where Nadyne changed his bandages, gave him a tetanus shot, and reviewed the day's schedule with him. Mercifully, his office appointments were light with only some suspected cases of whooping cough, measles, and bronchitis, mixed in with a few unspecified ailments and injuries, before his scant round of house calls in the afternoon.

Before the patients started arriving, the doctor called Sheriff Batson in Wewahitchka and reported what Jewel had told him about Lucky's moonshining activities and his relationship with this man Price. The sheriff thanked the doctor for the information and told him that he expected a report back from Tallahassee any day now. Hopefully, it would shed more light on exactly who this Lucky fellow was and where they might find him. The sheriff also told the doctor that the fingerprint photographs that the sheriff had sent in did match Martin's and Harvey Winn's, as expected, but no other prints on the hatchet or knife were detected.

The doctor was again disturbed when another Negro prostitute who had been beaten up turned up at his office that morning. This time, in addition to the bruises around the face and neck, the doctor had to set the woman's wrist that had been severely broken. He pleaded with her to tell him what had happened, but she wouldn't tell him anything. And, again, he promised himself that he would somehow find out who was responsible for this continuing brutality. This time, the doctor himself called the Port St. Joe chief of police, in whose jurisdiction the woman lived, but Chief Lane didn't seem any more interested than when Nadyne called, as if thinking to himself, so what's new. The truth was, both the doctor and Nadyne agreed, that no one in authority really cared that much if a colored whore was beaten. It was hard enough to prosecute a white man who was mistreating his own wife, let alone someone abusing a poor Negro working girl.

As the doctor was leaving for lunch and to make his afternoon house calls, he asked Nadyne to phone Mrs. Martin and tell her that he was going to drop by to check on Ronald that afternoon at around four and then, since everything else seemed under control, he was going home directly from there, unless he heard from her otherwise.

It was no easy feat to drive his car with his back so much in pain. He had to lean forward over the steering wheel with his nose practically on the windshield, like an old man who was having a hard time seeing the road. And he realized he must be proffering a rather strange sight as, later that afternoon, he pulled up in front of the lighthouse keeper's house where he found Harvey Winn on all fours, applying a thick coat of gray paint to his front porch, with a smokeless pipe still in his mouth.

"How ya doin', Doc?" he asked as he stood up and began digging in his pants pocket for a match.

"Fine, except for my back. How about you?"

"Oh, I'm okay. What happened to your back?"

"Long story," the doctor replied, "but it hurts like hell to lean back on the car seat, so I'm all hunched over the steering wheel like this. I was out this way so I thought I'd check on the Martin boy—see how he's doing."

"Good," the keeper said. "I think he's better. Sally sent him back to school today, and he looked okay when he got home a few minutes ago."

"Okay, I'll take a look. Good to see you again."

"You too. Take care of yourself."

Sally Martin, her flaming red hair in a wild, tangled ponytail, was standing on her front porch in a light, seersucker housedress, wiping her hands on a dish towel. She watched the doctor as he slowly climbed the steps with his black bag in hand.

"You look a little gimpy today," she said. "Anything wrong?"

He told her the story of what had happened to him at the Indian Pass Raw Bar after he had left her last Friday evening and the ensuing weekend at home being pampered by Nadyne and Jewel. He left out the part about the dream he had had about her, but he thought about it, particularly when the bright sun beamed through her thin, white dress as he followed her into the house.

Ronald's throat was no longer inflamed, either due to the administration of the doctor's special tea or by the simple passage of time. The doctor mussed the boy's sandy hair and sent him on his way.

Sally Martin poured the doctor a glass of sweet tea and invited him to sit with her on the front porch. It was another sunny day in paradise, as the residents sometimes referred to their forgotten little town, but a mass of clouds was gathering in the West that would likely deliver one of those brief afternoon showers that were so common in the area at this time of year. A cool breeze was blowing off the ocean, as the doctor watched a pair of dolphins swim northward along the coast.

"I feel terrible about your back," she said. "I feel somehow responsible for asking you to help me and you ending up like this. I'm sorry."

"Oh, don't be. You didn't ask me to go out there. I volunteered, as much out of my own curiosity, I have to admit, as of trying to help you. At any rate, it looks like I'm going to live, and hopefully the sheriff can track this Lucky guy down before he hurts anyone else. Are you afraid?"

"No," she said. "As I told you before, he had his chance, and he didn't take it. It looks to me like he doesn't like you nosing around though."

"No, I guess not. But what about you? How are you doing? Have you heard any more from that insurance fellow?"

"No, nothing more from the insurance man, but we're still doing okay. The Winns are helping us out, and so are the people from the church. Earl had one more paycheck coming, so we got that Friday in the mail, so as long as we can hold off the creditors until the insurance money comes through, we should be okay. I'm just hoping that the insurance guy completes his investigation soon and that everything is all right. Do you think that your being attacked has anything to do with the insurance investigation?"

"I don't know," the doctor said, as he removed his jacket and loosened his tie. "It seems like the insurance investigator thinks that your husband may have hired someone to kill him, but, again that doesn't really make sense to me. Your husband was apparently going to get this loan that his uncle had arranged, so I would think, with that, he would want to avoid his own death. And if he had hired this guy Lucky to kill him, why is he still hanging around? If Lucky is, in fact, the one who attacked me. Wouldn't he want to get as far away as possible if he had killed someone?"

"I don't know either," she said. "The more I think about all this the more confused I get."

"I know what you mean. It's all a mystery to me too. I hate to agree with that insurance guy, but there does seem to be something strange going on here. But, for the life of me, I can't figure out exactly what it is."

They sat for a while in silence, each trying to render some plausible explanation of what had happened. Finally, she said, "Would you like to stay for supper, Van?"

"I would love to," he answered, "but my back is killing me, and I'm afraid I wouldn't be much fun. I think I better get home and go to bed, but I'd like to take a rain check, if you don't mind."

"Any time," she said.

This time there was no doubt about what kind of kiss they shared. The doctor took a chance and put one hand on each side of her slim waist, just above her hips, and she put a light hand on the top of each of his shoulders, just above his wounds. Then they kissed for several seconds and continued holding each other like this until their lips separated and opened into wide smiles. Even though he still didn't dare to lean back onto it, the doctor's back seemed to be feeling much better as he drove along the meandering coast back to his empty house in quiet Port St. Joe.

Chapter Sixteen

The next morning Jewel again joined the doctor at the kitchen table for breakfast. She looked particularly pretty in a white cotton blouse and dark blue jumper, the doctor thought, as she sat across from him with her steaming cup of coffee in front of her and something obviously on her mind.

"Okay, Doc," she began. "Ready for the scoop on this Price guy that our friend Lucky works for?"

"Do I have a choice?"

"No, now listen. This is fascinatin'. This Price is the son of a famous doctor, who's dead now, named Roy Price from up north someplace who made a fortune selling these patent medicines that was supposed to cure about everything that you could think of. Ever hear of Dr. Price's Extract of Smartweed? The government made him take it off the shelf because it contained alcohol and morphine. Anyway, this older Price and his son, Elmer, who's a doctor too, made enough off these weird remedies that they bought up the whole island of St. Vincent. Now they got a bunch of houses on it, like Gator said, including two for a couple of colored families who live out there bein' butlers, and cooks, and maids, and such. One of them, Tom Black and his wife Peggy, and their three kids is related to my friend Pearl—Tom's her cousin. Well, Pearl, she got a tongue so long she can lick a skillet from the front porch, and she knows all about the place 'cause she helps out sometimes in the winter when a whole mess of the family comes down from up north. Accordin' to Pearl, they got a swimming pool where the family goes skinny dippin', and Tom has this big ol' horn that he blows reveille on every morning at eight o'clock, and they even have their own electricity that they get from a Delco generator that's run off gasoline."

"So what's any of this got to do with our man Lucky?" the doctor asked, with a mouth half full of blackberries and cream.

"Well, nothing, I guess. Pearl says don't nobody there know nothin' about any Lucky. The other colored family, the Washingtons, they help out with the whiskey makin', but they ain't heard of no Lucky neither. So I guess it's another dead-end, but it's sort of interestin', don't you think? Somebody so rich livin right here practically under our noses."

"It is, Jewel," the doctor had to admit. "But not nearly as interesting as how this man Lucky can live right here under our noses without anyone knowing one iota of anything about him."

"That's true. Everybody talks about how everyone knows everyone else's business in a small town, but when it comes down to it, there's a lot of secrets 'round here, ain't they?"

"Which reminds me, Jewel," the doctor said. "I need you to put your considerable investigating skills to work on another one of those secrets that's been bothering me. It seems that someone—I don't know who—has been beating up on colored prostitutes here in town. I can't tell you who exactly, because they're my patients, but I'd sure like to put a stop to it before someone gets more seriously hurt than they've already been. Any ideas?"

"Well, Doc," Jewel said. "That's sicker than a rabid dog. These prostitutes give you any clues?"

"No, they won't say a word. I think they're afraid, but I don't know of whom."

"Okay, Doc, I'll see what I can do. I don't know that I know that many prostitutes 'round here, but I bet you somebody I know does."

"I wouldn't take that bet on a bet, Jewel," the doctor said, placing his napkin on his plate and heading for the door.

"Oh, Doc," she said, as the doctor descended the back porch stairs, "the dishes, would it kill you just once? Y'all like talkin' to a rock."

It turned out to be another sunny, quiet day in Port St. Joe. The doctor saw a few patients in the morning, more than usual with one breathing problem or another. He wondered if the smoke from the new mill had anything to do with it. And then he made house calls in the afternoon. As he drove around the little town, he thought a lot about Sally Martin and what he seemed to be getting himself into with her. She was beautiful, that was for sure, in the kind of way that the doctor liked, not perfect, but sort of askew. In Sally's case, it was the juxtaposition of her natural, fair-skinned beauty with her simple, poor-folks way of dressing, in well-washed, worn cotton dresses that appealed to him. And, of course, there was her obvious neediness, which as a doctor, he was always a sucker for. What, if anything, Sally saw in him was more difficult to discern. He was sure from their last kiss that there was some genuine feeling there, that he just wasn't making all this up in his head—an old man's wishful thinking. But he was no prize for an attractive, young woman like Sally. She had her whole life ahead of her, it seemed to him, and he was nearing the end of his. So where to go from here, he was unsure. He didn't want to make a fool of himself by presuming too much and pursuing her too eagerly. On the other hand, he did enjoy being around her and wanted to help her in any way he could. Having experienced these romantic dilemmas before, he should have been better prepared, but he wasn't. He was falling in love again, and he couldn't seem to stop himself. Practically, he expected her to push him aside once she worked through her grief, confusion, and financial issues. But, amorously, he wanted their relationship to develop—into what, he couldn't guess. So he decided to continue pursuing her, slowly, cautiously, to see what transpired. He wasn't expecting too much, but he was hoping for a lot.

When the doctor arrived home that evening later than usual, he found it dark and empty. Jewel had left a note on the counter, saying that she had to take Marcus to a rehearsal for their church's Easter pageant and that his supper was in the oven, hopefully still warm if the doctor wasn't too late. He wasn't. The meatloaf and baked potato were still hot enough to melt the slice of butter that he topped the potato with and the meatloaf tasted great at any temperature. In fact, his favorite dish in the whole world was Jewel's cold meatloaf sandwich with mustard on fresh whole wheat bread. He also found some left-over radishes and green onions in the icebox, as well as a pitcher of sweet tea. And, on the windowsill, sat a pan of warm blackberry cobbler.

When he had finished overeating, again, he decided to get back into *Of Mice and Men*. Where exactly had he left it? The house was unusually quiet as he entered the dark parlor. He thought he heard a creak in the kitchen floor behind him. He froze, listening. This would not be a good time to panic, he told himself, as his heart raced. He held his breath and was sure he heard someone else breathing somewhere not too far away in the gloomy house. He had an unloaded shotgun in the bedroom closet upstairs. Why hadn't he been more careful? The front door was just a few steps away. Should he make a run for it? As he searched in the darkness for the light switch on the parlor wall, the hush was suddenly shattered by the raw ringing of the telephone on the kitchen wall. When the doctor finally located the light switch, he was sure he heard footsteps retreating from the house. He slowly returned to the kitchen with the phone's insistent ring still resonating. As he lifted the receiver, he looked out the window and saw nothing but the familiar shadows of the night. "Dr. Berber," the excited voice on the line said, "this is Mike Moorehead at the Port Inn. There's been an accident out on the pier here in front of the hotel. Someone just pulled one of our guests out of the bay and his head's bleeding something fierce. Can you come right away?"

"Yes, of course," the doctor said. "Exactly where is he?"

"On the shore, right under the boardwalk."

"I'll be right there."

With his car windows open to the night and the wind from the north, the doctor smelled that same strange stench that he had encountered at the new paper mill last week, rotting cabbage maybe. When he arrived at the rocky beach under the Port Inn boardwalk, he found a Port St. Joe patrolman kneeling beside a reclined body whose head was being held off the ground by another younger man whom the doctor did not recognize. The doctor rushed to the body as quickly as he could and found a vaguely familiar face. It took him a moment to identify it, but then he recognized the man as Harry Stanton, the insurance investigator, the prim little man he had talked to last week. Now here he was wet and shivering and with a bloody five-inch gash across the back of his head. But he was conscious and seemed to recognize the doctor, who leaned into his face and asked, "Where do you hurt, Mr. Stanton?"

"Uh, I'm not sure. I'm too cold to hurt right now, I think. My head, my head hurts a lot."

"Okay, let's see if we can get you up. I need to take you over to my office and clean that cut and warm you up."

They helped the man up and led him to the patrol car and drove the few blocks to the doctor's office. After the doctor had taken Stanton's wet clothes off him and wrapped him in a wool blanket, he shaved a patch of the man's thin hair, cleaned the cut, bandaged him up, and gave him a tetanus shot with the new vaccine. He seemed to look better, not so blue, so the patrolman asked him what had happened.

"Well, to be honest with you," Stanton said, as his color began to return, "I'm not exactly sure. After supper, I walked down the boardwalk from the hotel, and when I got to the pier I watched that over-the-water, merry-go-round swing that they have out there. Have you seen it? The swings really fly once they get going. At any rate, I was behind a rail and at what I thought was a safe distance from them when I was pushed hard from behind and went right through the rail and right into an oncoming swing. The next thing I know I'm in the water, trying like mad to get to shore. Luckily, some kid came along and helped me out. I can swim, but with all these clothes and my head throbbing, I was having a tough time. For a minute there I didn't think I was going to make it."

"You're sure you were pushed?" the patrolman asked.

"Yes, I believe so. I'm sure I felt something hitting me with some force. And I know I didn't jump in front of that thing."

"Okay," the patrolman said. "Doctor, what's the prognosis here?"

"He should be okay. I'd like him to stay here for a while until his clothes get dry, and then I'll take him back to the hotel. Then I'll check on him again in the morning to make sure nothing internal shows up."

"Okay, Doctor, thanks. Mr. Stanton, could you come into our office at City Hall tomorrow to make a formal statement? Meanwhile, I'll ask around on the pier to check if anyone saw what happened.

"Sure," Stanton said. "I'm leaving tomorrow, but I'll stop by your office on my way out of town."

"So you're leaving tomorrow?" the doctor inquired after the patrolman had left.

"Yes," Stanton said. "The company gives me a week maximum on these investigations. My week's up today. I suppose I could talk them into more time if I could convince them that I was actually pushed on purpose tonight and that it had something to do with my investigation. But, frankly, just between you and me, if I was pushed on purpose, which I suspect I was, whoever did it has done his job in scaring me off, if that was the motive. Because I'm scared. I don't need this. Legally, my company was responsible for paying the full value of the policy when the jury last week ruled Martin's death was at the hands of a party or parties unknown. I thought something fishy was going on, and I still do, so I convinced my supervisor to let me stick around to see what I could find out. And, at the end of a week, the only thing I've found out is that some moonshiner named Lucky was a friend of Martin's and he hasn't been seen since Martin's death. Not much to report. So I'll be on my way in the morning. There's another case in Pensacola they want me to look into. I'll advise the company to pay Mrs. Martin and let the local police and the sheriff worry about Lucky. If they find him, which I doubt, and can prove that he and Martin were in cahoots on this thing, then I'll be back. But, until then, I'll bid you and your inhospitable little town adieu."

The doctor wasn't sure if he should take offense with Stanton's remarks, after all the poor man had been through, but he did anyway.

Chapter Seventeen

The next morning when the doctor arrived at his office, he found the waiting room filled with the aroma of bay rum and Sheriff Batson sitting there, thumbing through an old issue of the *Saturday Evening Post*. Nadyne shrugged, as if to say "what was I to do?" and the sheriff asked the doctor if they could talk alone for a few minutes in his office.

Once in the doctor's office, the sheriff tipped back his hat, leaned back in his chair, and sighed, "I've been out at that new paper mill, and, Doc, I believe they're dumpin' something bad in the bay. It's all yellowy and green down there at the end of the canal. Never seen it like that before. You know anything about chemicals?"

"No, not really," the doctor said. "Just about medicines, but nothing about what they might be putting in the water. What do you think it is?"

"I don't know, but they're dumpin' something nasty in there, and, one way or another, I'm gonna find out what it is. If fish start dyin', I know the first place I'm gonna look. And the smell, Doc, have you noticed the smell of that place? That can't be healthy."

"Some say it smells like money," the doctor said.

"Yeah, money that's been pissed on by a shithouse full of greedy Yankees. Oh well, that's not what I came about anyway. I was just over at City Hall. I guess you know all about what happened to this insurance man Stanton last night, since you treated him?"

"Yes, he had a pretty nasty cut on his head. I'm going to check on him again in a few minutes."

"Yeah, well, I think I know who's responsible for that. I didn't tell Stanton, because frankly I don't trust the little fairy entirely, and I'd just as soon see him move on, unless, of course, we come up with something that proves insurance fraud and then you can bet your ass he'll be back here in a heart's beat. Until then, I think we can handle this on our own."

"So who do you think pushed him?"

"I told you, didn't I, that I'd sent a description of this guy Lucky to Tallahassee to see if it matched the description of any criminals or escapees they have on file there?" the sheriff said, leaning forward toward the doctor's desk. "And I finally heard back late yesterday afternoon. Seems there was a man named Anthony Lorenzo Lucilla, nicknamed Lucky, who escaped from the Florida State Hospital in Chattahoochee in thirty-four. He hasn't been seen or heard from since."

"Until now," the doctor said.

"Right, until now. This man Lucilla matches the description we have of the moonshiner at the Indian Pass Raw Bar. But what makes him even more interesting is the reason he was in the nut house in the first place."

"Which was?"

"When he was just a kid, sixteen, he supposedly got hopped up on marijuana down in Tampa and took an axe to his family while they were asleep. Murdered his mother, his father, his sister, and his two brothers. Didn't remember a thing. Said he had a dream where people tried to hack off his arms and slash him with knives and blood was dripping from an axe and other grisly stuff. In other words, a crazy son of a bitch. Apparently this Commissioner of the Narcotics Bureau, Harry Anslinger, blamed it all on the marijuana, but the doctors at the state hospital say Lucilla's insanity was most likely inherited. His parents, who ran a run-down sawmill down there, were first cousins, his daddy's uncle and two of his cousins had been committed to insane asylums, and his younger brother, Franklin, one of his victims, had been diagnosed a year before with something called dementia praecox, which, as it turns out, is the same thing our man Lucky was diagnosed with before he escaped. The doctors didn't even mention the marijuana in the report that I got. They just concluded that his problem was that he was crazier than a run-over dog with this dementia praecox thingamajig, and that he had definite homicidal tendencies. No shit. At any rate, it looks like he's our problem now."

"So now that you know who he is," the doctor said, "how do you find him? Before you answer that, let me give you an idea." And the doctor filled him in on everything Jewel had told them about Lucky and Elmer Price and his moonshining operation on St. Vincent Island.

"Yeah," the sheriff said. "When I heard that Lucky was selling moonshine, I suspected that we would find ourselves sooner or later at the doorsteps of the infamous Dr. Price. Here's the deal: he's been making moonshine on that island for the past fifteen years, some pretty good stuff I've been told. And I've been trying to stop him for almost that long. I've arrested several of his distributors in Gulf County over the years, but they always come back, like a bad penny, before you know it. Unfortunately, St. Vincent Island is not in my jurisdiction; it's in Franklin County, not Gulf County. And the sheriff there's in Price's pocket. Every time I complain to him, nothing happens. I've reported Price three times to the feds. The first time, they ignored me— nothing happened as far as I could see. The next time they sent a boat over there and somebody shot it up with a shotgun." Gator, the doctor thought. "And the third time, I was told to my face that Price and his operation was protected. That was the word they used, 'protected,' and I was wasting my time going after him. So I've given up on him. As long as he's not hurting anyone, I guess it's the feds' business if they don't want to collect any taxes from him."

"But now we have a case where someone has been hurt," the doctor said. "And it's likely that someone working for Price is responsible, not only for Martin's death, but also Stanton's head, not to mention by back."

"Here's my problem, Doc: The feds ain't gonna help us out on this. The sheriff in Franklin County won't do a thing either. And the man, Price, wouldn't talk to me even if I did have jurisdiction, which I don't. So if Price does know something about Lucky and his whereabouts, I'm dumbfounded on just how to get it out of him."

"I see your point, Sheriff," the doctor said, just as befuddled, until he suddenly thought of something. "Hey, Gator Mica knows this Price," he said. "Why don't we ask Gator to talk to him. If he's determined to protect Lucky, then he won't tell Gator anything, but, if, on the off chance, he really doesn't care that much about him, maybe he could tell Gator something that could help us find him."

"Hmm." The sheriff thought for a minute. "I'm not so sure I want Gator involved in this. I know you and him are buddies, Doc. And nothing against him because he's an Injun, or anything like that, but you gotta admit the man's got a temper. Say Price crosses him and Gator decides to lay him out. Then we have whoever's protecting him down here lookin' for us. And my sense is that these people are pretty important, a lot more important than you and me, Doc."

"What if I went with him? To make sure he stayed in line. This Price's a doctor, like me. Maybe we'd get along."

"The man's a moonshiner too, Doc. I'm sure he'd be all civilized and polite when you talk to him, but I know these guys. They'd just as soon shoot a man dead than to give up a penny or a drop of whiskey."

"Well, I can't say I'm too excited by the prospect," the doctor said, "after what happened to me at the Indian Pass Raw Bar, but it doesn't seem like we have too many options here. This man keeps hanging around, and what you've just told me about him makes me more certain that we better do something soon before something else really bad happens."

"There is a chance that if all of us stopped poking around that this Lucky nut might just disappear, you know. I can't understand why he's hanging around anyway. If he killed Martin, why didn't he just take off? Go to the next town and terrorize them."

"Are you willing to take that chance, Sheriff?"

The sheriff thought for a few seconds. "No," he finally said, "I guess not. It's against my better judgment to let you two go over there, but, like you say, it doesn't look like we have too many good options here. But for Christ sakes make sure Gator behaves himself and don't take any unnecessary chances. The last thing we need around here is another murder. Just be careful, will ya?"

When the doctor got home that evening, he was pleased to find Jewel and Marcus still there. Jewel had prepared a supper of fried cod cakes topped with homemade corn relish, fresh pole beans, and dirty rice. After dessert, warm bread pudding, Marcus was again exiled to the kitchen to clean up, and Jewel and the doctor repaired to the back porch to sip a bit of moonshine and enjoy the night air. The doctor knew he shouldn't, but he did tell Jewel about what the sheriff had discovered about the mysterious man Lucky Lucilla. She was fascinated by all the gory details, as the doctor knew she would be, but she was not too happy to hear that he planned to join Gator on a fact-finding excursion to St. Vincent Island.

"Have y'all taken leave of yo' senses?" she scolded. "Let Gator go by hisself. He don't need you, Doc. After what you been through with your back, you don't need no more aggravation. The sheriff's right, the man may be a doctor, but he's still a moonshiner. You're the one who said to leave this up to the sheriff, so why ain't you takin' your own advice? Might as well play hob with the hoe handle."

"Jewel, I don't have the slightest idea what that means, but I'll be fine. I'm curious about this man now. It won't hurt to ask him a few questions. He's not going to kill us for that."

"I hope not, Doc," Jewel said. "I sure hope not."

Chapter Eighteen

The healing holes in the doctor's back made it difficult for him to get a good night's sleep. He realized that he must have been used to sleeping on his back more than he thought because he would wake up suddenly in pain every time he turned over on it, which turned out to be several times a night. This aggravation coupled with his usual morning angst made starting a new day even more miserable than usual.

His despondent mood didn't seem to affect Jewel, however. She was as cheery as usual and seemed to be genuinely concerned when she asked the doctor how he was doing this morning.

"I'm okay, Jewel, except I'm old and my back hurts, but nothing's infected, so I should count myself lucky, I guess—no pun intended."

"No pun taken, Doc."

"Where'd you get this cantaloupe? It's good, nice and ripe and sweet and juicy."

"Liz Wright, the note said. Waitin' for me on the porch this mornin.' "

"Liz Wright? Do you know who that is?" the doctor asked.

"No, don't know her from a hole in the wall."

"Hmm," the doctor considered. "Any news on those colored prostitutes I asked you about?"

"No, Doc, I'm afraid not. Not yet, but I got the word out. Somethin'll turn up."

"I hope so. I dread having to patch up another one of those women."

Over his cantaloupe, ham, grits, and black coffee, the doctor read the weekly edition of the St. Joe *Star,* which reported that the new Martin Playhouse was nearing completion just down the street from his office. Florida's junior U.S. senator, Claude Pepper, had been in town on Monday to give a speech, according to the paper, touting his accomplishments in Washington that were benefiting the area, including $500,000 for the restoration of the oyster industry, $300,000 for the purchase of surplus fish, and a loan for $7,000,000 "to peg the price of naval stores and permit the orderly marketing of gum rosin and turpentine," whatever that meant. The rest was mostly tame local news and various advertisements.

The doctor finished reading the newspaper and eating his breakfast and was already out the door when he heard Jewel's annoyed voice. He couldn't be sure with his poor hearing, but he thought it had something do with "those damn dishes."

When he arrived at the office, Nadyne, smelling faintly of talcum powder as usual, reviewed his schedule with him and reminded him that he needed to make his weekly visit to the Wesley Home. So before he started seeing patients, he called Sally Martin and asked her if he could cash in that rain check she had promised and stop by after he had completed his rounds at the nursing home. She seemed pleased with the idea, and the doctor found himself thinking about her the rest of the day.

When, after completing his depressing, weekly face-off with death at the Wesley Home, the doctor pulled in at the San Blas Lighthouse, he found what he assumed was the back end of Harvey Winn, sticking out from under the hood of a faded old white Oldsmobile touring car.

"Hey, Doc." The keeper waved, as his head emerged from under the hood. "Heard you comin' way up the road. Welcome back."

"Thanks. I was in the neighborhood, so I thought I'd check in on the Martins. See how they're doing. Everything okay with you and your family?"

"Can't complain. Aside from what happened to Earl, it's been a nice spring. I've been trying to keep an eye on Sally and her kids too, and they seem to be doin' okay. As I said before, I think the world of 'em, and I'd do about anything for that gal Sally."

"I understand. They do seem like a real fine family. It's too bad that they're without a daddy, but they seem to be doing okay under the circumstances."

"Yep, I reckon so," the lighthouse keeper said as he tapped a wad of Prince Albert tobacco into his pipe.

Sally met the doctor at the front door with a kiss on the cheek and asked him to keep her company in the kitchen while she prepared supper. She offered him a glass of sweet tea, and he sat down at the kitchen table and watched her move gracefully about the room in a flowery cotton shift.

"Better than that stuff you had me give Ronald, huh? How's your back?"

"A lot better. Thank you. It's still sore, but I guess I'll live. What are you making? Can I help?"

"Well, let's see. Pretty simple, as usual. I've got a big hen that Harvey gave us roasting in the oven stuffed with a bunch of things from the garden, fresh herbs and chunks of lemon and garlic, alongside some other vegetables from the garden: sliced up young carrots, onions, and potatoes. That's about it except for a cucumber salad with tomatoes, onions, and vinegar that's already made and in the icebox and those oatmeal cookies cooling over there on the windowsill if the kids haven't stolen them all by now."

"Doesn't sound simple to me. Speaking of the kids, how are they?"

"They're fine. Upstairs doing their homework, I hope. I'll have them set the table in a minute. We have a little while before the chicken's done. You want to sit out on the porch. The oven's really heated up this kitchen."

They again sat on the rocking chairs on the front porch and enjoyed the sun lighting up the distant clouds. The doctor loosened his tie, and Sally pulled her hair back into a long ponytail, fastening it in back with a rubber band.

"I have some good news for you," the doctor said and then told her about the insurance man, Stanton, and his swim in the bay and his assertion that he was giving up his investigation and advising the insurance company to pay her the full value of her husband's policy.

"Oh, that's wonderful news," she exclaimed, getting up and giving the doctor a big hug and another kiss on the cheek. "Did he say when they would pay it?"

"No, but I got the impression that it would be soon."

The doctor also told her what the sheriff had reported about the true identity of the mysterious man Lucky and his relationship to the moonshiner Elmer Price and about his plan to visit him.

"Van," she said when he had finished giving her all the news, "do you really think it's a good idea for you to go see this moonshiner Price with this maniac Lucky still running around? I mean moonshiners are notoriously harsh, from all I've heard, and this Lucky guy is liable to do anything, it sounds like to me. Can't the sheriff or your friend Gator handle this? It seems to me you've done more than enough already. Next time you might not be so lucky."

"No pun intended," the doctor said for the second time that day. "Don't worry. I'm taking Gator for protection. He knows Price and we'll be careful. That chicken sure does smell good."

"Oh, it's got to be ready now. It's time to eat," she said, as she rose from the rocking chair. "I see talking to you about this is not going to do any good."

The meal, as before, was fabulous. The children were more at ease and talkative this time, and the doctor thoroughly enjoyed hearing about their long walk to the bus stop each morning and their teachers and their friends and their after-school activities. In fact, once they got started, it would have been hard to shut them up, not that he really wanted to. He was enjoying it all too much, even if he wasn't alone with their mother. When the children did finally finish clearing the table and doing the dishes and went upstairs to prepare for bed, the doctor and Sally did have a chance to sit alone for a while on the front porch and enjoy the starlit evening together.

"I've applied at a few places in town," she said, "as a typist. It's about the only skill I have, but I'm hopeful that something will work out."

"I'm glad you're staying here, and please let me help you if you need me to put in a good word with anybody. I'm sure I'm not liked by everyone in town, but I've treated enough of them for free or for goods and services that I've got more than a few favors outstanding I would hope."

"Thank you, Van. You've been so kind throughout this whole ordeal. How can I ever repay you?"

He took a chance and raised his eyebrows in a mock leer. "Well," he said, "let me think about that."

"Shame on you," she whispered.

They sat there on the porch together, not saying much more. The bright light from the evening's stars was disturbed only by the intermittent light from the tower above them. The doctor reached over and held her hand. It seemed so small and moist and warm. When, after a while, he got up to leave, they kissed goodnight, holding each other with urgency, pressing their bodies together until she felt him hard against her belly. Blushing, she pulled away and said, "Please come back again soon. And, Van, please be careful, okay?"

Chapter Nineteen

The doctor awoke early on Sunday morning, April 3, and he felt stiff and achy, as usual, and especially old. Since it was the weekend, he was alone in the house, and the streets of Port St. Joe were quiet. The choir of birds outside was intoning one of its familiar morning hymns, but everyone human, it seeemed, was beneath the spire of one sanctified church or another, except for him and a few other local heathens and infidels who, despite the toll of the steeples' bells, had still not risen from bed.

The doctor had been forced by his parents to attend the St. James Armenian Apostolic Church in Watertown every Sunday, but when he had moved away to go to college at Colgate University in upstate New York, he had stopped going altogether. He was all "churched out," he told people when they asked him about his lack of devoutness, but the truth was he did not believe in God anymore, if he ever had. There was a force keeping everything together, he believed, but no single God or religion. At Colgate, he had taken a Religions of the World course, and the closest religion to what he believed was Taoism, a sort of indefinable non-religion that he imagined to be like the American Indian's Great Spirit and matched the ambiguous way he thought about such things when he took the time to contemplate them. When at med school at Tufts in Boston, a fellow student had suggested that he was a humanist since he was in medical school and studying to serve humanity, the doctor had considered this and ultimately refuted it since, in truth, he did not hold the overwhelming majority of humanity in very high regard. He had respected a few individuals in his life, but the mass of evidence only demonstrated to him man's continuing inhumanity to man.

The truth was that whatever made the birds sing outside his window this morning, the feeling of holding Sally Martin close, Jewel's cooking, well, Jewel herself, and the few other friends he had were about all the doctor really believed in anymore, and not much else.

When the doctor had finished showering, dressing, and eating the bacon and eggs that he had made for himself, he heard the familiar sound of a car sliding to a stop in the shell driveway at the back of his house. No car that he knew of possessed as poor brakes as Gator Mica's 1927 Chevy Capitol pickup, so the doctor knew well before Gator stepped on the porch who was interrupting his peaceful Sunday morning.

"Mornin', partner," Gator greeted as he entered the house. "Happy birthday!"

"Good morning, Gator. Thanks. I suppose Jewel told you."

"Yep, and, if I ain't mistaken' it's a big one, like 65, right?"

"Right, I'm afraid so, but Roosevelt's new Social Security Act doesn't make us old-timers eligible for benefits until nineteen forty-two, so I've got four more years to go before I can even think about resting."

"Too bad, but at least you can rest today. It's Sunday and it's your birthday, so it's time to go fishing."

"Oh, Gator, that's a great idea. I could sure stand to get out of this town for a little while. You're on. What do I need?"

"Not a thing, partner. Just yourself and a straw hat. This is my treat," Gator said, escorting the doctor to his old pickup truck that already had Gator's long glade skiff loaded and tied down in the back.

It was another brilliant spring morning as Gator drove north out of Port St. Joe on State Road 71 through the little, county-seat town of Wewahitchka, past the old brick courthouse with its stately white portico supported by four high Southern-mansion-style columns. The doctor didn't see any cars parked on the square this morning, so he guessed that Sheriff Batson and his deputies were either out patrolling or off duty for the day.

Just outside of town, they turned off on an unmarked dirt road to Dead Lakes, through a thick forest of longleaf pine, magnolia, and bald cypress, and backed the pickup up to the shoreline, scattering a menagerie of turtles, snakes, and alligators into the still, green water. The lake had been formed years before, the local lore went, when sandbars created by the current of the Apalachicola River blocked the Chipola River, backing up the water to form the lake. Later, a flood of salt water temporarily replaced the fresh water, killing the cypress trees and leaving only dead stumps that now rose majestically out of the waters into the morning mist like mysterious, primordial totems.

Gator and the doctor wrestled the sixteen-foot skiff into the water, and Gator pulled the starter rope on the little one-and-a-half-horsepower Briggs engine that Gator called a "hothead" until the engine sprang to life. Gator expertly turned the hothead mounted at the stern to maneuver them slowly through the imposing cypress stumps into a shallow cove where Gator cut the engine and dropped a makeshift anchor, a rusty coffee can filled with concrete and attached to a hemp rope, over the side of the skiff. The boat was less than a yard wide and only about ten inches deep, made from native cypress especially for fishing and alligator hunting in the Everglades and swamps and shallow streams and lakes like this one. Gator sat on a narrow shelf at the stern of the skiff and the doctor on a wider seat near the bow. In between them, on the boat's flat bottom, was Gator's usual cargo: two cane fishing poles, a rifle, and three five-gallon lard cans, one containing bait, another holding waxed-paper-wrapped bologna sandwiches and deep-fried cod balls, and the third filled with big chunks of ice and brown bottles of Spearman beer. Gator baited the hooks with earthworms and handed the doctor a pole and a bottle of beer. A great blue heron waded and fished patiently nearby, and a hawk, outlined against a cloudless sky, eyed them suspiciously from the top of a tall, vine-covered cypress stump.

As they each waited for a bite, the doctor told Gator about what the sheriff had found out about Lucky and his dilemma about approaching Price and his volunteering Gator's assistance in questioning the moonshiner. Gator, as the doctor guessed, was eager for the adventure and to introduce Price to the doctor.

"I'll get over there in the next couple of days and see what I can set up," Gator said, as he cast his line into a shady hole near the shore. "I think you'll like him, partner. He ain't all haughty like a rich, Eastern-educated doctor, no offense, and he ain't all mean like you'd think a moonshiner to be. Maybe just a little formal, but other than that he seems like good people. And his island is great, the wildest, most wonderful place you'll ever find—not ruined by the turpentiners, or the lumbermen, or the paper people. Besides the deer that's everywhere, there's wild hogs that grow as big as a quarter ton, even bigger giant sea turtles that crawl up onto the dunes to lay their eggs, and fish—I've caught flounders off the shore there that are a yard across. You already know 'bout the oysters—the best in the world. And there's five freshwater ponds over there where I've caught a single largemouth black bass big enough to feed me for a week. And great flocks of widgeon and pintails that one shot from a shotgun will rain big ol' birds on you without even aiming. It's truly a wonderland—what Florida was like before the white man spoiled it."

"Whoa, I got a bite here," the doctor interrupted as he fought what turned out to be a nice, fat, five-pound bass. Gator helped haul it into the boat and off the hook and onto a stringer.

They continued fishing, occasionally moving the boat into one or the other of Gator's secret inlets, until the doctor interrupted their silence. "Ever been in love, Gator?" he asked.

"Yeah, once, before I came here. When I was campin' in the Everglades. Fell for a Seminole gal named Mai—pretty and passionate as a panther. I would've married her 'cept she wouldn't hear of livin' anywhere 'cept the city. Said us Indians had enough of bein' poor and livin' off the land and these was new times. We needed to get civilized. 'Civilized'—that's what she said. I couldn't see it, workin' like a slave for a white man so I could live in a cramped little cottage surrounded by people who live so close together they know when you change your mind. No, not for me. 'Cause I loved her so much, I told her I'd consider movin' into town, but after about a year or so and I'm still campin' in the woods, she left me for another man. Then me and him got into it one night in a bar in Florida City, and I had to get out of town fast. And the fact that they were talkin' about turning most of the Glades into some kind of big ol' national park sealed it. I put on my travelin' shoes and skedaddled out of there and finally ended up here after a while. I like it here now, but I expect the same thing would happen if I took up with some other gal. Nobody really wants to live out in the swamps with the snakes and skeeters 'cept a few of us crazies, and I guess I'm just too ornery to change my ways—sort of used to 'em by now. So, here I am."

Then Gator caught a skillet-size bluegill, and the doctor told him about Sally Martin, and how he had met her, and how sweet and pretty she was, and how they seemed to be getting along, and how he thought about her an awful lot, and how he wanted to spend more and more time with her. It just sort of all spilled out, since he had not yet talked to anyone else about her.

"Sounds like you're in love to me," Gator said when he had finished his story.

"Well, maybe I am," admitted the doctor. "I'm not so sure. I do like her and I do want to see her some more, but it seems like maybe I'm just too old for this kind of thing. You would think I'd had enough of it, like you, Gator, that I'd learned my lesson by now. Except for my first wife, Annie, I've found love, if you want to know the truth, to be about ninety per cent of the time more trouble than it's worth."

"Yeah, as my ol' daddy used to say, 'son, if it's got tits or tires, sooner or later you're gonna have trouble with it,' but maybe this time it'll be different, partner. She's sounds like a real nice lady."

"Maybe so, Gator," the doctor said. "I sure hope so. I guess I'll find out soon enough."

The two spent most of the rest of the day floating from shallow cove to swampy inlet, drinking beer, fishing, and relaxing. Before the afternoon was over, they had caught two more good-sized bass, another bluegill, and three tupelo bream. And then, when all the sandwiches and cod balls and beer were gone, they pulled anchor and headed home.

Chapter Twenty

Later that afternoon, when Gator and the doctor arrived back at the doctor's kitchen, they found it full, or nearly so. Jewel and Marcus were there, as well as Jewel's blues singer boyfriend, Gabriel White, and his diminutive friend, Reggie Robinson.

"What are y'all doing here?" the doctor asked, knowing full well what Jewel had conjured.

"Happy birthday, Doc!" she said, giving him a playful hug and peck on the cheek.

"Happy birthday!" the rest chimed in.

"Thank y'all, and thank y'all for coming," the doctor said. "What's cooking, Jewel?"

"You tell me. What did y'all catch?"

Gator held up the stringer of fresh fish. "Ooowee," Jewel exclaimed. "That's finer than frog hair split four ways. Gator, you start cleanin' them right now. Not in my kitchen. Outside on that old bench. I want 'em skinned and filleted. Gabriel, you start slicin' them radishes, onions, and asparagus. Reggie, you shell them peas. Marcus, scrub them new creamer potatoes that someone left on the porch this mornin'. I don't want to see a speck of dirt on 'em. The cake's already in the oven, and I'll start on the cracklin' corn bread now. Doc, since you the birthday boy, pour yo'self and everybody else a glass of Gator's moonshine and let's get this party started."

The little kitchen swirled into a hurricane of activity. Marcus begged for the doctor to put a record on his record player, and the doctor obliged by selecting a new 78 by Sonny Boy Williamson called "Good Morning Little School Girl" that he knew Gabriel would like. The doctor asked Gabriel how his career was going.

"Well," the big bluesman said. He was more than six feet and looked sharp in his starched white shirt and denim overalls. "I think I told you the last time I was here about winnin' first prize in that folk festival they have up in St. Louis."

"Yeah, I remember," the doctor said. "And what's this Jewel was telling me about you meeting some kind of Yankee folklorist?"

"Uh-huh, that's right. While back, this young white fellow named Lomax and a colored woman named Hurston over in Eatonville, they recorded me and Reggie for the Library of Congress. Come to find out, this Hurston woman, full name's Zora Neale Hurston, is a writer and she's just written this hell of a book you gotta read, Doc, called *Their Eyes Were Watching God* about a poor colored gal trying to get by right down here in Florida."

"What else? You've been awful quiet, Reggie, as usual," the doctor prompted.

"Oh, then we be ramblin' like usual, pickin' up work where we can," Reggie answered.

"Tell Doc about what you been doin up in New York City," Jewel coached, turning away from her mixing bowl to give the bluesman a knowing wink.

"Well, 'cause of the Library of Congress recordings," Gabriel answered, "I've been up to New York City and worked in some plays with one of the Negro Units of the Federal Theatre Project that Roosevelt set up awhile back as a part of his Works Progress Administration to give work to poor out-of-work actors and musicians like me. So I been in a couple of plays up there. We did a thing called *Swing Mikado,* a bluesy version of Gilbert and Sullivan's operetta that I had a small part in, and then we did a Caribbean version of *Macbeth* that they were calling the *Voodoo Macbeth* directed by this young fellow named Orson Welles. Real talented, creative guy. That's about it. They don't pay much, and the work is sort of sporadic, so Reggie and me still tryin' to pick up a few bucks playin' the blues. We're hopin' to get signed on to do a radio show with a guy I met named Richard Huey, but I'll just have to wait and see about that. What's new with you, Doc?"

The doctor told him that his life was not nearly as exciting as Gabriel's, but that there had been a murder recently and he was about to mention Sally Martin, which he had been avoiding bringing up to Jewel because he didn't want her to stick her nose into it just yet, when their supper seemed to be reaching a critical point, with everything coming clamorously together at once.

"Okay, Marcus, set that table," Jewel instructed. "Let's see, I count six. Bring a couple of chairs in from the porch and don't worry about matchin' the plates. I think we only got four that match anyway. And pour some sweet tea from the icebox. The moonshine can wait till after supper. I ain't gonna have a bunch of drunk ol' men sittin' 'round my table."

While barking instructions to Marcus, Jewel was frying long, thick strips of bacon in a big, black cast-iron skillet and then placing them on a towel to drain, periodically cursing and slapping the backs of men's hands that were attempting to steal a sample. At the same time, while the bacon was cooking, she was mixing up a big bowl of stone-ground cornmeal with pinches of baking soda, baking powder, salt, a couple of beaten eggs, and two cups of buttermilk. When all the bacon was cooked, she poured some of the hot grease into the cornmeal mixture, drained off the rest into a waiting Kerr-Mason jar, grabbed a handful of the cooked bacon and crumbled it into the bowl, and then, when the thin layer of grease in the frying pan began sizzling and was just starting to smoke, she dumped the cornmeal batter into the hot pan, instantly smothering the spitting grease and triggering the savory scent of a perfect Southern supper. The full pan then went into a hot oven, and Jewel was on to the next task, emptying Marcus's clean creamer potatoes into a large sauce pan of boiling water, and then blanching the asparagus slices and peas in another pan of boiling water. While they were cooking, she put another large cast-iron skillet on the burner and added some of the remaining bacon grease, turning the flame up high. When they had turned bright green, she dumped the asparagus and peas into a strainer in the sink and then emptied them into a large floral bowl with the sliced onions and radishes, mixing them all together with a splash of bacon grease and liberal pinches of salt and pepper, and topping them all with another handful of crumbled bacon. When the grease in the frying pan was hissing to her satisfaction, she started carefully laying the fish fillets in it, squeezing a bit of lemon juice and sprinkles of salt and pepper on each side. While the fish fillets were cooking, she took the tiny creamer potatoes from the sauce pan, drained them in a strainer, returned them to the pan, and began crushing them with a potato masher. When they were thoroughly smashed, she added salt and pepper, and a dab of butter. Then, with the rolled-up hem of her apron, she pulled the cornbread from the oven and put it on the windowsill to cool. She told the men to sit down and then she started passing bowls and platters around the table. While all the dishes were being passed, she inverted the frying pan of cornbread onto a plate and sliced it into generous sections and then placed it with a saucer of butter in the middle of the table.

"To the doctor," Gator said, raising his glass, "May he live a long life, full of love, and die a fast death, with no regrets."

"I'll buy that," the doctor said, as everyone tapped glasses.

"Pass the cornbread, please," Marcus said. And everyone ate.

The main topic of conversation around the table was where the best fishing holes in Gulf County were located. Gabriel and Reggie played their music at night and during the day they liked to fish and hunt. Gator was clearly the expert on where the best spots were and on which pieces of land not to trespass or poach on. Since the troubadours did not have a boat, arrangements were made for Gator to take them out in the bay in his glade skiff to do some saltwater fishing.

"I'll guarantee you some good eatin,' " he said. "We've got everything around here: trout, redfish, pompano, mackerel, kingfish, grouper, and even tarpon if we go far enough out."

Finally, Jewel tired of the conversation and ordered them all to get out of her kitchen and go out on the back porch while she helped Marcus clean up the mess. Gator poured everyone a glass of moonshine and passed out Cuban Partagas cigars, while Gabriel broke out his guitar and started singing. His friend Reggie never said much, but he always carried an old pasteboard valise filled with a fanciful assortment of instruments to accompany Gabriel with. Depending on the song, Reggie would produce another guitar, an old clay jug to blow the base line with, a couple of pairs of spoons to keep time, a homemade diddley bow to pluck along with the tune, a harmonica to provide either harmony or melody as needed, or he'd just keep the beat with his hands on the table or on himself with a syncopated hambone beat. Gabriel's voice was a loud, high tenor and his flat-top, slide guitar playing, slick and quick and economical, with no extra flourishes or flashiness. His repertoire was vast, from simple blues and folk songs to popular show and movie tunes that he had learned by ear. If you could hum it, he could play it. According to Jewel, audiences loved him, and he made good money in tips by being able to play anything that they requested.

Soon Jewel and Marcus joined them. Gator danced with Jewel, and then Marcus broke in and danced with his mother. Gabriel sang a slow blues ballad called "The Motherless Child," and, while Reggie sang and played his battered, old guitar, Gabriel put down his guitar and danced with Jewel, swaying together as one to the mournful tune. And with another round of moonshine, even the doctor danced, spinning Jewel blithely around as Gabriel sang "Tone the Bell Easy," while Reggie tapped out the mad rhythm with a pair of spoons.

Then Gabriel and Reggie took a break, and Jewel went in to get the dessert. It was a big, round, three-layer, white coconut cake with fluffy white frosting and freshly grated coconut sprinkled on top—the doctor's favorite. Mercifully, Jewel withheld the candles, but everybody sang happy birthday to him, and the doctor was predictably embarrassed and suddenly tired. Gator insisted on one more round of moonshine to go with the cake, and Gabriel sang a few more songs.

Then, sometime later, after Gabriel and Reggie played "Careless Love," Jewel announced that she had to get Marcus home to bed, since tomorrow was a school day and he, and she, and the doctor, for that matter, had to get up early and go to work, unlike lowlifes like Gator, Gabriel, and Reggie who could sleep until noon if they wanted to. The doctor thanked everyone as they left the house and, with a quick nip of morphine, was sound asleep before their cars were barely out of the driveway.

Chapter Twenty-one

Early the next Wednesday morning, the doctor found Gator Mica parked in front of his office, slouched in the driver's seat of his pickup truck, smoking a Partagas cigar and digging dirt from under his fingernails with a pen knife.

"Top of the mornin' to you, partner," he greeted the doctor. "I talked to the notorious moonshiner Dr. Price yesterday, and he says he'd be honored to see us this afternoon if you can make it."

"Come on in, Gator. Let's check with Nadyne to see what's up today."

"Nadyne, what's happening?" he said, as they entered the office.

Nadyne looked up suspiciously over her thick glasses. She had once confided in the doctor, even though "it isn't any of my business," that she didn't entirely approve of the doctor's friend, Gator, and didn't understand why the doctor put up with him. He was always dirty, didn't have a paying job, and had a penchant for showing up unannounced at any time of the day or night. In other words, she just thought the doctor deserved a friend with a little more class than Gator Mica. The doctor had just smiled and laughed. He had to agree that his friend lacked class in the usual sense of the word, but he had told Nadyne that all the crude characteristics that she had attributed to Gator were, after all, the same as those of a faithful dog—man's best friend, he had reminded her.

As it turned out, the doctor's late afternoon was free, if he could somehow pull himself away from old man Jenkins with his deteriorating case of gregarious dementia. "See you at four at your place?" he said.

"I'll be waitin'," Gator replied and was out the door before Nadyne could scold him about tracking in mud with his grimy boots or the doctor could ask him what the appropriate attire was to meet an infamous moonshiner. Then he picked up the phone and called Sally Martin to see if he could stop by on his way to Gator's. She said of course and told him that if he got there before four the kids would not be home from school yet. The doctor told her that he'd be there by three, at the latest. The pleasant thought of some private time with Sally Martin would keep him going the rest of the day. Then he called Jewel, while he was thinking about it, and told her that he would probably not be home for supper, since he knew Gator would expect them to eat at his place.

Nadyne informed him that this morning he was to see a suspected case of bronchitis, Mrs. Cochran's gout, the Smith kid's possible broken finger sustained while playing catch with his father last night, Marge Flemming's monthly pregnancy checkup, and another nasty cut at the paper mill that had just been reported. In the afternoon, Nadyne had him scheduled to visit Katherine Ferguson, whose baby he had delivered in the Panama City Hospital a few days before; Ben Runnels, who was dying of lung cancer; Jerry Windsor's measles, Marilyn Frazier's high fever, and, of course, George Jenkins's advancing senility.

By the time he reached the San Blas Lighthouse, he was ready for a nap, preferably with Sally Martin, and not some high seas adventure with Gator Mica and his bootlegger friend. When he pulled up in front of the lighthouse keeper's house, he found a sweating Harvey Winn at the side

of his house, with a long-handled axe in his hands, splitting a chunk of
bleached driftwood.

"Hey, Harvey, what's new?" the doctor asked, as the keeper pulled a
handkerchief from his back pocket and wiped his brow.

"Not much. Sally's been cleaning house all day, so I suspected she
might be havin' visitors."

"Yep, she sure is. How's the lighthouse business?"

"Lookin' up," the keeper answered as though he had been asked this
question a thousand times before. "Got a right, bright future, I'd say."

"Very good," the doctor laughed. "Keep making light of it."

Sally Martin was waiting for him in her kitchen and she looked
stunning. "Do you like it," she said, spinning around for the doctor in
a form-fitting navy blue dress. "It's brand new. I have a job interview
tomorrow at the new Kenney Mill, so I splurged."

"You look gorgeous. They'd be crazy not to hire you."

"Well, we'll see. Would you like a glass of tea?"

"Yes, thank you. I'm sorry that I'm later than I said. I had a devil of
a time getting away from a patient who loves to chat forever. But here I
am, finally, with only a little time before the kids show up and I have to
meet Gator. We're going over to see this moonshiner Price today to see if
he knows anything more about this Lucky Lucilla."

"Oh, Van, I wish you wouldn't go. I just don't see what good can
come of it. Do you really think you're going to find out anything new?"

"Well, to be honest with you, I doubt it," the doctor admitted, "but I
don't know what else to do. It just doesn't seem right to sit here and wait
for this crazy man Lucky to strike again. If the sheriff had any jurisdiction
over there, I'd forget it in a minute, but since he doesn't and no one can
seem to think of an alternative, I guess we're going to give it a try."

She stepped forward and wrapped her arms around him as if he
were a soldier going off to war. And even though he wasn't, and was

only crossing Indian Pass for a simple visit with a fellow doctor, he took advantage of her attention and put his arms around her, massaging with both hands first her shoulders, then her back, and then slowly inching lower down her backside until her firm, little ass was filling his hands. As usual, she smelled of gardenia and Ivory soap. He kissed her lips and continued rubbing her, pulling her into him, as he moved his lips to her neck. Soon their hips were moving together in an easy rolling rhythm and their kisses became more fervent. As he was sliding his left hand onto her breast, they heard voices outside—the children coming across the front yard.

"Can I see you Friday?" he panted, trying to catch his breath as he backed away from her.

"Yes, of course. Come for supper," she said. "And, please, Van, be careful."

It was only a few miles from the lighthouse to Gator's camp, which was hidden off an unmarked dirt road not far from Indian Pass, the quarter-mile channel that separated the mainland from St. Vincent Island and connected Apalachicola Bay and the Gulf of Mexico. A few feet beyond a large decaying live oak that had been uprooted by the 1935 Labor Day hurricane, the doctor found the single-lane dirt road. He drove down it until he saw the rusted-out fifty-gallon oil can in a ditch on the right side of the road. Just beyond it was the left turn to Gator's house which was hidden behind a sandy hammock in a dense grove of scrub oak, live oak, and palmettos.

The house was actually an old houseboat that Gator had bought from a man for ten dollars. Gator had propped it about six feet up on cypress stilts on a little knoll so that he could see just over the dunes to Indian Pass and the blue expanse of the Gulf of Mexico beyond. When the doctor pulled in behind Gator's pickup, Gator, in a white T-shirt and bib overalls, appeared at the door and waved him in. The houseboat/house was only about seven feet by fifteen feet, with a window on one side overlooking the dunes and the channel and a window on the opposite side that looked out onto Gator's vegetable garden. Gator had a cot in one corner, with a mosquito net hanging over it, and a four-hole wood-burning stove covered with cast-iron cookware in another. He sat on boxes strewn about the floor and ate off the top of an old trunk. Wooden orange crates were stacked against the crowded walls filled with provisions: sacks of flour, sugar, rice, beans, and coffee cans everywhere. The mostly faded blue Maxwell House cans were filled with everything but coffee, from screws, shotgun shells, nuts, and bolts to a wide assortment of arcane devices whose uses only Gator might decipher. Gator had dug a well in the backyard, but the water that he drew from it was often brackish, so he usually had to haul fresh water from town in five-gallon lard cans. There were a couple of kerosene lanterns for light at night and the bathroom was a one-hole outhouse just beyond the garden.

"You ready, partner?" Gator asked as he picked up a lard can in one hand and his rifle in the other.

"As I'll ever be," the doctor said, following Gator down the sandy path to the beach. Gator had hidden his skiff between two high dunes, and they labored mightily to pull it down the flat beach to the water. By the time they arrived there, the doctor's back was aching and his white cotton shirt was uncomfortably plastered to it, but Gator didn't even need a rest, so the doctor had to hurry to clamber into his usual seat in the bow, as Gator pushed them with one swift shove into the sudsy surf. The Briggs engine started on the second try, and they were off across Indian Pass.

"What we're gonna do here," Gator explained, "is to cross the channel and then go around the island due east into St. Vincent Sound and then south parallel to the shore about twenty-five yards out. That way we should avoid the shoals but stay out of the open ocean. This old skiff is great in the swamps, but it wasn't built to be out here. Lucky the weather is good. Price's place is at the far southeast corner of the island. We could've sailed directly across Indian Pass and then hiked on the beach around to his house, but that would've taken forever and we'd be eaten alive by the time we got there, if not by skeeters, then by alligators and snakes. Throw me a beer from that lard can in front of you, will you? And help yourself. This shouldn't take too long, as long as this ol' hothead keeps on churnin'."

The little engine did keep on churning, laboring noisily against the swift current of the narrow pass. Once across the pass, they motored slowly along the island's coast in clear view of its wide, empty beaches and undulating white sand dunes. Brown pelicans sailed along beside them, periodically diving bill-first to snag a fish in the shallow surf, and a half dozen bottlenose dolphins played next to their boat for a while and then passed them by and disappeared somewhere out to sea. Gator pointed out the sights: Big Bayou, Sheepshead Bayou, and in the distance the northwestern tip of St. George Island and Horseshoe Cove. Inland, near the freshwater ponds, they saw ospreys nesting in the high snags of dead pine trees and young eagles testing their wings and soaring gracefully over their heads, then looping lazily back to their nests.

"Sure is pretty," the doctor said above the sputtering hum of the engine.

"The way it's meant to be," Gator agreed, squinting against the afternoon sun and guiding the hothead with one hand and holding a cold bottle of beer in the other. "The way it's meant to be."

Chapter Twenty-two

After about half an hour of cruising along the island's edge, the doctor and Gator saw a long dock that extended about thirty feet out from the shore. Tied to it were a classy, little white sailboat with its sail neatly wrapped around its mast and a long, mahogany Chris-Craft inboard motorboat large enough to hold at least a half dozen people. Gator steered his humble skiff to the end of dock, and they tied it up there. Then they walked along the dock until it ended in a white sand path that led them between two high dunes behind which stood a complex of buildings, including four houses, a barn, and a spacious tin-roofed toolshed.

They walked to the largest house and were met at the front door by a glum butler whose skin was almost as dark as his formal wool suit, undoubtedly the man Jewel had told them about. The house was very quiet and smelled of furniture polish and something good—pot roast?— baking in the oven. The butler led them through a long, dark hallway to a room at the back of the house where a frail-looking old man sat in a stuffed brown leather chair behind an expansive oak desk. The walls were lined from floor to ceiling with pine shelves filled with books, except for a huge window on one wall that afforded a dramatic view of the ocean. The old man stood when the butler showed the doctor and Gator in and introduced himself. "Elmer Price," he said, extending his bony hand, "but most people call me El. Please have a seat. Gator tells me you're a doctor?"

"Yes, as are you, I understand."

"That's right. University of Buffalo College of Medicine. Eighteen ninety-one."

"Tufts," the doctor responded. "Ninety-eight."

"A fine school. What brings you to these parts?"

"Well, after med school, my wife and I moved to Nashua, New Hampshire, where I operated a clinic, specializing in eyes, nose, and throat problems, but after a few years, the winters got to be too much for us, so we moved south, first to Cochran, Georgia, and later to Lynn Haven City, Florida, before I came to Port St. Joe a few years ago. And you, Doctor?"

"I, like you, am from the North—Buffalo, New York, to be precise. My late father, Roy Price, founded a medical company there that you may have heard of called the People's Dispensary Medical Association. It produces a number of patent medicines, including Dr. Price's Golden Medical Discovery, Dr. Price's Favorite Prescription, and Dr. Price's Pleasant Purgative Pellets, as well as publishing the *People's Common Sense Medical Guide.* Thanks to the popularity of these products and others, my father was able to buy this beautiful island in nineteen-oh-eight, and our family has been coming down here every winter since then. And since my retirement from the company a few years back, I spend all my time here now. The closest thing to heaven on earth—especially compared to a Buffalo winter."

"Well, I guess that means that Gator is the only native then, albeit twice removed, from Oklahoma and the Everglades," the doctor said.

"Yes, and thanks be. Gator keeps a close eye on the sound and has been a good friend of mine for some years now. Which reminds me, I'm being remiss as a friend and host here by not offering you a drink. What'll it be, fellows? I have the usual taxed varieties, as well as, as you might expect, my own specialties: corn, cane, or honey whiskey. The corn is similar to a fine vodka, the cane goes down like a good Cuban rum, and the honey, some call it metheglin, is more along the lines of a sweet, after-dinner liqueur. Which would you prefer?"

"I'll have my usual, the cane," Gator said. "That's the one you're used to, partner," he added, nodding to Dr. Berber.

"The same," the doctor said.

Price rose with some difficulty from his leather chair and shuffled to an enclosed shelf in the bookcase behind him. Inside were a variety of bottles and several large, cut crystal glasses, three of which he filled with the clear liquor.

"Sit," he commanded Dr. Berber and Gator, as he slowly rounded his desk and presented the drinks. "To more friends," Price toasted, raising his glass, "and less need of them."

After they had touched glasses and Dr. Price had crept back to his chair behind his desk, they sat and sipped the smooth homemade rum.

In a moment, Dr. Berber broke their brief reverie. "Dr. Price," he ventured, "if you don't mind me asking, how did you get into the liquor business?"

Dr. Price did not answer but instead peered solemnly back and forth between Gator and Dr. Berber, as if trying to decide how to deal with these two interlopers. Finally, he stared at Gator and said, "Gator, I've known you some time now and I know I can trust you. The good doctor here I've just met, so I'm somewhat hesitant to divulge all my trade secrets. No offense, Doctor. So before I go any further I'm assuming that you're vouching for Dr. Berber's discretion and assuring me that no a word spoken here will leave this room."

"Don't worry 'bout a thing," Gator assured him. "Dr. Berber is just trying to help the widow Martin find out who killed her husband. He has no interest in hurting you or your business. After all, he enjoys the fruits of your labors just as much as the next fellow."

"Maybe more," Dr. Berber smiled and added, taking a long swallow of Dr. Price's illegal elixir.

"All right then," Dr. Price sighed. "In the interest of medical fraternity, if nothing else, I will trust you, Doctor. I will, of course, deny ever having this conversation. And I am sure I don't have to remind you that I know very well how to find you both . . . whenever I like."

"Doctor," Dr. Berber said, "I assure you that your secrets are safe with Gator and me. And if I'm overstepping my bounds, please, of course, feel free not to answer my questions, which, as Gator said, are only for the purpose of helping the widow and her family, nothing more."

"All right. It started out innocently enough, I guess, as a hobby during Prohibition. We had these chemists who worked for the medical company, and we gave them the challenge of concocting some beverages that we could make easily down here in our toolshed, using readily available local produce. Since plenty of corn, sugar cane, and honey are produced around here, that's what they used. And they did such a good job that we started selling it in the area. People seemed to like what we made, and, when Prohibition ended in thirty-three, the demand remained. Our whiskey was cheaper and better tasting than the commercial varieties. Unfortunately, during this period, the demand for patent medicines continued to decline, what with the Depression raging and the Federal Trade Commission on our backs. Now they're about ready to pass this new, even tougher federal Food, Drug and Cosmetic Act that will make it even harder to earn a buck with patent medicines. The liquor business has helped us take up the slack and maintain some semblance of the standard of living that we've grown accustomed to, without having to sell our timber to those St. Joe Paper Mill bandits. They and the lumber mills have ruined much of north Florida, but we're doing our best here to save what little we can."

"How wide is your distribution network now?" the doctor asked, as he sank deeper into the big, soft, leather chair.

"We cover most of northern Florida, some into southern Georgia and Alabama, but not much farther than that. Because of the nature of the business, we have to keep somewhat of a low profile, as you know."

"As for your distribution around here, do you happen to have a fellow named Lucky who works for you?" Dr. Berber asked.

"Ah yes, Gator said that you were looking for this Lucky, who may have something to do with the lighthouse keeper's murder," Dr. Price said. "Yes, we did have a man named Lucky who worked for us around this area, but he seems to have disappeared."

"When was that?"

"Well, now that you mention it, I don't believe we've seen him since the murder."

"Do you have any idea where he lives or where we might find him?"

"No, I'm afraid I don't. We run a strictly cash-and carry-business here, and we don't keep track of where anyone lives. We delivered a truckload of whiskey to Lucky every Wednesday night at the Indian Pass Raw Bar. He paid us cash on the barrelhead for it, and neither of us asked any questions."

"How long have y'all been working together?"

"Oh, I'd say about three or four years now. As I recall, he came to our man in Apalachicola about the possibility of his selling out of the Indian Pass Raw Bar and a couple of other places. He was a strange, scruffy-looking fellow, but we gave him a trial run and he caught on. He's never given us any trouble, always has the money, and always shows up. But he was real quiet, never said much, and, I've asked around, none of our men who delivered to him know a thing about him."

"Could you give us a description of him?"

"Well, I only met him that once, when I hired him, but I recall that he was, as I said, a bit ruffled, weird look in his eye, dark, tall, curly-haired. He may have given me his full name then, but I don't remember it if he did. I usually look for someone like him in this business. Someone who doesn't say much, keeps to himself, cautious, and looks like he's afraid of something or someone."

"Any idea where he could be?"

"Now? No, not a clue. I've asked the delivery men, but they say they always just find him waiting in the back parking lot of the Indian Pass Raw Bar. He must have a home somewhere, but I don't know where."

"Any chance he could be hiding out here on your island?"

"Here?" Dr. Price put his left hand to his temple and thought a moment. "Hmm, that's another good question, Doctor. I've often thought that our little piece of paradise would make an excellent hideout for someone. Not particularly for this fellow, mind you, but there is plenty of wild fruit and game to eat, there's fresh water in several ponds, and heaven knows we have enough thick pine, live oak, and yaupon forests to easily hide anyone who really wanted to be hidden. Of course, there are the mosquitoes, alligators, snakes, and even a few panthers to deal with, but if a fellow could put up with them, he might never be found. So, yes, to answer your question, I'd say there is a chance that he may be hiding around here somewhere, but we've not seen hide nor hair of him so far."

"Thank you, Doctor," Dr. Berber said, extricating himself with some effort from the plush chair and extending his hand. "You've been most helpful. If you do happen to run into him, could you let Gator know? I would hate to have anyone else meet the same fate as poor Mr. Martin, the assistant lighthouse keeper."

"Of course, Doctor, I'm sorry about the entire situation. If this man Lucky is responsible for someone's death, I'm afraid, since he worked for me, that it reflects on me and our little operation here, and that's the last thing I want. As I said, we try to avoid anything that draws attention to ourselves, so if we find the man, you can rest assured that he will be dealt with severely." With that, he heaved himself out of his leather chair and headed back toward the liquor shelf.

"One more round," Dr. Price insisted, filling each man's glass again. "To good women and sworn secrets," he proclaimed, raising his glass high. "May they always be carefully kept."

Chapter Twenty-three

After two more rounds, Gator and the doctor stumbled back in the gathering darkness to the skiff, still bobbing lazily where they had left it. The trusty Briggs engine finally came to life on Gator's fourth pull and they were off along the island's coast in the way that they had come. There was no moon this clear night, but as the sky darkened it began to fill with stars. When they were out of sight of the Price dock and compound, the sea around them took on a bright, violet phosphorescent hue. The doctor raked his hands through the waves to create streaks of shining brilliance. The island's dunes soon became dusky shrouds as more and more stars appeared. As the hothead puttered along and the waves slapped the skiff, it was only Gator and the doctor, the sea, and the stars.

As it grew darker, the starlight melded together into one brilliant blaze of luminescence. And below them the phosphorescence of the sea lit their way. It was like being in one vast, dazzling chamber of radiance, the doctor thought.

"Toss me a beer, will you, partner?" Gator said, steering the skiff attentively along the coast.

The doctor, now mesmerized by the sparkling spectacle of the night, removed the lid from the lard can and reached in without looking. He felt something round, like a bottle of beer, but suddenly it started moving. Before he could decipher exactly what it was, he pulled it out of the lard can, without thinking, and held it at arm's length up to the bright night light to see that he was grasping something alive, warm, wriggling, and round instead of a cold bottle of beer.

"Holy shit! It's a water moccasin!" Gator yelled.

The doctor instinctively flung the serpent, its mouth now gaping open wide and white, into the sea, but in his haste, his right foot slipped and knocked over the lard can. Out slithered a writhing mass of black, pent-up anger— dozens of long, quick, crawling cottonmouth water moccasins.

"Holy fucking shit!" Gator shouted.

"Now what?" the doctor hollered, scooting as fast as he could to the farthermost front edge of the boat.

"Abandon ship!" Gator commanded, as he turned off the hothead and performed an odd, lopsided swan dive into the ocean. The force of Gator's pushing off the boat into this awkward dive so jostled the skiff that the doctor, who was now standing as far forward in the boat as he could, tumbled backward over the bow and into the cold water with his friend.

"Nicely done, partner," Gator laughed as he clung to the stern of the boat.

"Yeah, well, you're no Johnny Weissmuller yourself," the doctor gasped, hanging tight to the bow line and treading water.

Then the doctor heard a strange, sort of choking noise from Gator's end of the boat. "Gator, are you all right?" he asked.

And then the choking noise turned into a cough, and then a weird chortle, and then a full-blown howl of laughter that echoed across the sea.

"What's so goddamn funny?" the doctor shouted, which only sent Gator into another spasm of laughter.

"I only wish," Gator said between outbursts, "that I'd had a Brownie camera to capture the look on your face. Oh, God, I can't stop laughing. It's like. Oh, Jesus. It's like you'd just delivered the devil's first-born baby."

"Yeah, well, I've never seen terror like I saw in your eyes when you caught a look at those snakes heading your way. You looked like you just saw the Titanic hit the ice."

"Yeah, and I was going down with it."

They floated there for a while, listening to the hushed scurrying about onboard, until Gator finally was able to contain his laughter.

"You think those snakes can climb out of the boat?" the doctor asked, which only set Gator off again into another round of uncontrolled laughter.

"If they can," Gator laughed, "I hope they climb out at your end."

"Seriously, Gator, what are we gonna do here? I'm getting cold, and water-logged, and I'm not going back in that damn boat no matter what."

"Ah, come on," Gator said, "be a sport. Jump back in there and get me my rifle and I'll pick 'em off one by one."

"Get your own goddamn rifle," the doctor replied.

"Okay then, let's see," Gator said with one hand on the stern and his head peaking out just above the water. "How 'bout we kick our way to shore and hope none of them moccasins climb over the side after us, and then when we get to shore, we quick dump the boat over and empty the snakes out on the beach."

"Well, if you say so. I don't have a better plan. But if I get bit by one of those things, just remember to give my body to medical science, okay?"

This started Gator laughing again, but the doctor refused to give him the satisfaction of asking exactly why, particularly since it was all too apparent by now just how ludicrous their situation had become. Here they were, after all, two fully clothed, grown men splashing around in the Apalachicola Bay surf in the middle of the night with a flimsy swamp boat filled with a tangled mass of agitated water moccasins. This was definitely not how the doctor had envisioned his end.

When the doctor finally felt the sandy bottom beneath his feet, he climbed up the beach pulling the bow line as Gator pushed the stern out of the waves. When the boat was completely out of the water, Gator quickly disengaged the Briggs engine and carried it up the beach out of the way of the incoming tide. By now the snakes, no longer lolled by their gentle ride on the waves, had become a fiery cauldron of hissing rage, crawling madly over each other in a crazed attempt to vacate the boat.

"Okay, partner, on three," Gator said. "You grab the stern, and I'll take the bow and we'll flip this baby over and run like hell. One, two, three . . ."

As they turned the boat over, out dropped Gator's dripping rifle and the now-empty lard can, which bounced aimlessly down the beach, and, of course, the writhing glob of snakes. Then the boat was firmly on the sand upside down with the snakes below it. Standing back several yards from the upturned skiff, they watched, waiting for the onslaught of enraged vipers, as nothing happened. "Okay," the doctor said after a while. "Now we've got a bunch of frenzied water moccasins trapped under our boat. What next?"

"Uh, good question," Gator said. "I hadn't really figured that out. Any ideas?"

"You're the great outdoorsman."

"Well, I suppose at some point," Gator said, "they might burrow their way out, but that could be all night. I guess we have no choice but to flip the damn boat back on its bottom and the let the moccasins loose."

The doctor thought for a moment. "Okay, if you say so. On three. One, two, three . . ."

Then, when the boat was quickly righted, the snakes all suddenly scattered, fighting madly to get free of one another and the boat, and the doctor and Gator racing wildly in opposite directions to stay out of the way of the scurrying serpents. In the bright starlight, Gator had found a piece of driftwood and picked it up and was now hammering anything black that came his way. The doctor had taken off his water-soaked shoes and was ready to defend himself against anything approaching on the sand. As it turned out, the water moccasins were far more interested in finding cover than they were in attacking the two sailors, and so they soon had slithered off into the dunes and sea oats and, at least for the time being, were out of sight.

When it finally appeared that the coast was all clear of them, the doctor and Gator carefully crept back to the boat and searched it thoroughly before loading the empty lard can and Gator's gritty rifle and relaunching the sandy skiff back into the surf. Gator retrieved the hothead and, knee-deep in the waves, reattached it to the skiff. But after repeated pulls, it just wouldn't start. The doctor was preparing to be marooned there on that desolate beach with the water moccasins all night long, a thought that was about to push him into panic mode, when finally, after Gator had cursed and fiddled with it for the umpteenth time, the engine turned over, and they were on their way.

It must have been nearing midnight—the doctor wasn't sure since his pocket watch's crystal had fogged over and Gator never carried a timepiece—when they dragged the skiff ashore and hid it in Gator's hiding place between the dunes. They were both tired and still saltwater-soaked when they reached Gator's camp. Gator found some old cotton work clothes for the doctor to change into, and even though they were several sizes too large, they were at least warm and dry. After Gator had changed, he carefully reached into the old trunk that he used as an icebox and withdrew a burlap bag of oysters and cold bottles of Spearman beer for both of them. By the light of two kerosene lanterns, Gator shucked the oysters, and the doctor halved some lemons to squeeze on them.

And then, as they sat on the upturned boxes slurping their supper, Gator broke into laughter once again. This time, the doctor joined him.

Chapter Twenty-four

Both the doctor and Gator agreed that it was not Dr. Price's style to sabotage their visit with poisonous snakes and that the elusive Lucky was more likely the culprit. The theory that he was hiding out somewhere on St. Vincent Island and had seen them arrive and then planted the water moccasins on their boat seemed to be more plausible than Price directing one of his workers to mete out some sort of serpentine retribution for their nosiness. At least that's the theory that the doctor espoused to Sheriff Batson the next afternoon when the sheriff came to visit him again in his office.

"Well," the sheriff said, rocking back in his chair, with a toothpick lodged in the side of his mouth, "I guess that puts us back to square one. Let's see what we've got here. This moonshiner Price admits to employing this man, Anthony Lorenzo "Lucky" Lucilla, or at least someone fitting his description. Lucilla is an escapee from the state funny farm where he was admitted for hacking to death his entire family in much the same way that our friend Earl Martin was killed. Speaking of friends, this Lucky Lucilla nut was apparently some kind of friend with Martin. And every since Martin was murdered, no one has seen Lucky. But you and Gator Mica, and possibly Dr. Price, think he may be hiding out on St. Vincent Island. Does that about sum it up?"

"Yes," the doctor said, "but I still don't understand why this Lucky Lucilla would want to kill Martin if Martin was his friend."

"Who knows, maybe some dispute. Most murders are committed by friends or family members. Maybe Martin owed him money and he wasn't paying."

"Yeah, that's Gator's theory," the doctor said. "But if Martin was about to get this loan from the bank that his uncle had arranged, wouldn't that have made it unnecessary for Lucky to kill him. If, as our insurance investigator friend . . . what's his name?"

"Stanton," the sheriff said.

"Yeah, Stanton, if Stanton's right and Martin hired Lucky Lucilla to kill him, why would he have to do that if Martin was getting a loan. Presumably Martin, or his family, wouldn't need the insurance money when the loan came through. Or if Martin owed Lucky money, wouldn't Lucky have been better off to wait for the loan to come through so he could collect whatever Martin owed him?"

"Maybe Lucky didn't believe Martin was getting a loan. Maybe he had heard every excuse in the book why Martin couldn't pay and how the money was coming and how he only needed a few more days. Maybe he just got tired of hearing these excuses and decided to make an example out of Martin for any others he had made loans to?" the sheriff said.

"Yeah," the doctor said, "but if Martin was an example, who was he an example for? I mean Lucky doesn't seem to be sitting in the back parking lot of the Indian Pass Raw Bar anymore, doling out loans or even moonshine for that matter. Except for occasional acts of violence, mainly directed at me it seems, the man appears to have disappeared from the face of the earth."

"Good question, Doc. I wish I knew. Whether there was a loan or not, it looks to me like something went terribly wrong with Lucky and Martin's so-called friendship. If it's true that this axe murderer has been living amongst us for the past few years without much notice and then suddenly snaps and butchers Martin, then something must have set him off, but I don't know what."

"Why do you think he's after me?" the doctor asked.

"I don't think it's anything personal, Doc. I just think he doesn't want you nosing around. I think he wants this whole damn thing to go away, and it looks like to him that you're not letting that happen."

"But I still don't understand why he just doesn't leave town. Why should he stay around here? He must know that if he does, someone will find him sooner or later."

"I don't know," the sheriff said. "He must be waiting for something, but I don't know what."

"There is, of course, the chance that we're all barking up the wrong tree here," the doctor said, "that this Lucky fellow had nothing to do with Martin's murder and all these bits of evidence—Lucky's past, his friendship with Martin, his description, his disappearance—are all coincidental or can be explained in some other way not connected to Martin's death."

"Are you suggesting that someone else may have been responsible for his murder?" the sheriff asked, his voice rising in astonishment.

"I don't know. I just think maybe we should consider the possibility, that's all."

"Okay," the sheriff said, "who do you have in mind then?"

"Well, nobody in particular. I don't know. Just an idea. At this point, the only thing I know for certain is that I'm pretty tired of being attacked, whether by this Lucky fellow or anyone else."

"I can't say as I blame you, Doc. I shouldn't have let you go over there in the first place. I think the best thing is for you to let me handle this on my own from now on, okay?"

"Sure," the doctor said. "I'm more than happy to do that, but I don't see how exactly you're going to handle it if we're right and Lucky is hiding out on St. Vincent Island. You've already said that the island is in Franklin County, out of your jurisdiction, and that the sheriff over there isn't going to do anything to disturb Price and his operation, so where does that leave you as far as capturing this guy before he decides to hack up someone else?"

"Good question, Doc. This ain't the movies, so I ain't gonna round up a posse or anything like that. I think the only thing to do right now is wait until he makes his next move and then see if we can somehow trap him. Ain't nobody goin' over to that jungle on St. Vincent to root him out anyway. That's like diggin' your own grave—what with panthers, and alligators, and wild boars, not to mention snakes, moonshiners, and maybe a crazy, axe-wielding nut job, all just waitin' for you to enter their lair. Uh-uh, ain't gonna happen."

The doctor had to agree. He knew he wasn't going back there anytime soon. And, as much as he would have liked to be a hero to Sally Martin by capturing her husband's killer, he was becoming convinced that if he didn't mind his own business he himself was soon going to end up just like the hapless, hacked-to-death assistant lighthouse keeper. At this point, he didn't know what else to do anyway. In fact, the only thing he really wanted to do right now was to get this day over with as quickly as possible so he could go home and take a double dose of morphine and go to bed. He still ached all over from last night's exertions, and he wanted to forget about Earl Martin and Lucky Lucilla and go to sleep.

Chapter Twenty-five

Jewel was not pleased when the doctor told her about Price and the water moccasins. She blamed Gator, the sheriff, and the doctor. So the doctor was getting Jewel's version of the cold shoulder this Friday morning, meaning that she was not being her usual cheery self—which suited the doctor fine; he would rather read the newspaper anyway than to chat with Jewel at this hour of the morning. This week's paper was a big one, what the *Star* was calling the Progress Edition. It was filled with stories and advertisements touting the town's success and particularly the full operation of the $7.5 million St. Joe Paper Company, which was being hailed as "the South's newest and finest paper mill."

The doctor was still stiff from his Wednesday night swim in Apalachicola Bay, so he was slower than usual in getting up from the kitchen table, which gave Jewel a chance to chide him at the start of what otherwise looked to be another unremarkable spring day.

"Doc," she said, "stay away from the sheriff, stay away from Gator, and stay away from this whole Martin thing. It ain't yo' business. You understand? Enough is enough. I swear, I could just wring yo' neck sometimes. And for God's sake, just for once, would you put your dishes in the sink. I've done told you fifty eleven times now. I don't mind washin' them for you, but it's just plain rude not to at least offer to help out once in a while."

"Okay, Jewel," the doctor said, hobbling out the door, "when I'm feeling better. I can hardly move this morning."

Nadyne, as usual, reviewed the day's schedule with the doctor when he arrived at the office. Afterwards, when he had already seen the Leary boy about his recent asthma attack and Mrs. Wilder about her reoccurring nausea and headaches, Nadyne interrupted him to let him know that a bruised colored woman without an appointment was in the waiting room. When she entered the examination room, the doctor was shocked and disgusted by what he saw. It appeared that she had been beaten badly over every inch of her face, neck, and arms that the doctor could see. Both eyes were almost swollen shut and there was a deep cut on her lower lip. What once must have been a pretty face was no longer.

"What's your name?" he asked her.

"Yolanda," she whispered.

"Yolanda what?"

"Yolanda Brown."

"Yolanda, are you injured anyplace else besides your face, neck and arms?"

"Yes."

"Where?"

"My breasts," she said.

"May I look at them? I'll have the nurse join us."

"Okay," she agreed.

The doctor asked Nadyne to come in, and he examined her bruised and battered breasts.

"Who did this?" he asked her.

"I can't tell you."

"Why not?"

"'Cause I'll get hurt worse if I do."

The doctor then went into a long and what he thought was a convincing plea to the woman to tell him who had beaten her, how she needed to tell him so it wouldn't happen to other women, and how she needed to help before the man killed someone. She wouldn't budge. So he and Nadyne patched her up the best they could. There wasn't much they could do about the bruises, but the woman was lucky that she didn't have any broken bones. The next woman might not be so fortunate, the doctor thought.

The sight of the poor woman hung over him like a shroud for the rest of the day. Again, he called Chief Lane at the Port St. Joe Police Department, but, again, he was met with indifference. "We'll do what we can, Doc," the chief said, "but unless one of these gals signs a complaint, we ain't got much to go on."

He wondered if it would do any good to call Sheriff Batson. His jurisdiction was only in the county outside of the towns like Port St. Joe that had their own police forces, but it wasn't all that clear-cut, the doctor knew. Sometimes the jurisdictional lines were murky and the two law enforcement departments worked together on certain issues, although the doctor was ignorant of exactly how they decided when to cooperate and when not to. So he phoned the sheriff, but he was told that Sheriff Batson was at the St. Joe Paper Company mill for some unspecified reason. He left a message, but didn't give the dispatcher any details.

When later that afternoon, having completed his weekly, depressing visit with the town's geriatric generation at the Wesley Home, he pulled up in front of Harvey Winn's cottage, he found the keeper sitting in his rocking chair on the front porch, whittling something in his lap with a polished pearl-handled penknife and smoking his pipe.

"Looks like we're going to get a shower this afternoon," the doctor observed.

"Yep, reckon so. How's it goin'?"

"Good. How are things with you?"

"Okay, I guess. Nothin' much new to report," the lighthouse keeper said. " 'Cept that I'm thinkin' of retirin' sometime soon. I've been at this for more than twenty years now, and with Earl bein' killed and Sally and the kids movin' on, I don't see much future in hangin' around anymore."

"I'm sorry to hear that, Harvey. You still afraid then that the man who killed Earl might come after you next?"

"You're damn right I am. No use takin' chances if you don't have to, that's the way I look at it."

Sally Martin was waiting for the doctor on her front porch and was, like the keeper, rocking in her rocking chair and looking out to sea. Unlike the keeper, she looked beautiful, in a sleeveless white blouse and homemade gingham skirt.

"Come join me," she said. "The children are making us supper. Tell me about your voyage to St. Vincent Island."

The doctor told her the story, now already told twice before to Jewel and the sheriff, but he had to admit that, no matter how he spun it, the tale made him and Gator sound more than a little foolish, out there in the ocean, half-drunk, fending off a boatload of vicious vipers.

"Oh, Van, it must have been awful," Sally said without a hint of a smirk. "Are you okay?"

"Yes," he said. "More humiliated than anything. But what's new with you?"

"I have some good news," she said.

"Yes," the doctor said, pulling the other rocker over close to hers, "what is it?"

"The insurance check came this morning. I went to town already and put it in the bank. We're not rich, but at least I won't have to worry anymore. If I don't get that job at the mill, we'll still be okay for a while, but I should know about the job in the next few days."

"That's great," the doctor said. "You'll be moving into town then?"

"As soon as I can find a place."

"I'm looking forward to that. Are you?"

"Yes," she said. "I am. I grew up as an only child out on a poor little farm in the Texas panhandle and then I met Earl and moved here. It seems like I've been lonely and independent all my life. Our nearest neighbor in Texas was over ten miles away, so, when I wasn't doing chores, I spent a lot of time in my room by myself playing with dolls or reading books. So coming here was much better, at least in comparison, or so I thought. Then Earl sort of abandoned us here with the Winns, who are nice enough but, after a while, maybe too much of a good thing, as they say. How about you? Were you ever lonely?"

"No," the doctor said, trying to remember. "Not as a child. I had two little sisters, Lora and Sona, and they seemed like they were always around. And we lived in Watertown, Massachusetts, near Boston, in a close Armenian neighborhood, so there was always a bunch of Armenian immigrant children just like me to play with. So I can't say I was ever really lonely, except, of course, after Annie disappeared. I was terribly lonely then, until I remarried."

"You had a happy childhood then?"

"Happy? Oh, I don't know. I guess it was happy enough. My parents fought all the time when I was young, and I hated that. My father was a janitor at the Perkins School for the Blind, and he didn't make very much money. My mother was more educated, but she didn't work and stayed at home with us kids. So they were always arguing about money. We never seemed to have enough of it. I remember telling myself that I would never fight like that with my wife, and I didn't when I got married, maybe even to a fault. An occasional fight might have been better than me trying to avoid one at all costs. But that's water under the bridge, as they say. The only time I remember being really unhappy back then was when a friend of mine, a little girl named Rachel Manuelian, died of polio when we were twelve. She was my first love, and, even though we were very young, I missed her terribly. I guess I still do, as well as Annie, and Carrie Jo, and Jennie, and my parents—and my sisters, even though they're still alive, but I hardly ever see them or talk to them anymore. Now that I think about it, it seems like I've gone through my entire life losing people. They die or they just go away. And then I'm alone again and missing them. And then, like a fool, I try to replace them, try to fill the hole in my heart that they've left empty."

"Supper's ready!" a child's voice came from the kitchen.

The doctor could not believe what they had prepared all by themselves. John, the oldest boy, had again been successful at fishing from the beach and caught enough fresh pompano to grill and serve the family. The oldest girl, Earlene, had boiled some of Sally's salt potatoes and baked fresh cauliflower and melted pecorino cheese over the top of it, and, for dessert, the two little ones, Ronald and Roseanne, had peeled and sectioned some local Satsuma oranges and sprinkled them with freshly grated coconut. It was delicious, as usual, and the doctor ate more than he should have, as did Roseanne, who ended up moaning in bed with stomach pains. All the children looked at the doctor as if he should do something, so he examined her, but, since the child did not have a fever and seemed all right in every other respect, he surmised that the pain was would gradually dissipate on its own. Unfortunately, Sally felt bound to comfort the little girl, so the doctor said good night and promised everyone ice cream if they would come to visit him in town. Only Roseanne did not seem thrilled.

Chapter Twenty-six

Thankfully, the doctor's weekend was relatively uneventful. There was only one emergency call, on Saturday morning. Ben Crowley fell out of a tree and broke his ankle. The doctor applied a temporary splint and told the boy's parents to take him to the Panama City Hospital for a plaster cast. So the doctor slept most of the rest of the weekend and by Monday the pain from both of his investigator injuries, as the doctor thought of them, the soreness in his back from the oyster rake attack and the stiffness from his workout with Gator and the snakes, had subsided. He had had only one dream that he remembered and it had something to do with the sheriff and a fierce battle with someone who looked like how he imagined Lucky Lucilla to look, but, try as he might, he could not remember the outcome.

"Good mornin', Doc," Jewel greeted, as she placed a plate of shrimp and grits and a slice of honey dew melon in front of him. "Mind if I join you?"

"Of course not, Jewel, as long as I don't have to listen to a lecture about staying away from the Martin case and clearing the table."

"Oh, it's the *case* now, is it?" she said. "Mister big-time private eye."

"Whatever, Jewel. You know what I mean. What's up?"

"Well, I have this friend, Brenda Walsh. She's the mother of this boy, Willie, who's in Marcus's class at school. Real nice lady, but sometimes she don't know whether she's washin' or hangin' out. Well, anyway, turns out she lives next door to a woman named Yolanda Brown. And, well, we, Brenda and me, we have coffee together sometime on Saturday mornin' when her husband's still asleep 'cause he works nights, you know. Anyway, Brenda she tells me that this Yolanda come around all beaten up bad Friday mornin' and how she can't understand it 'cause Yolanda ain't married or nothin', so it can't be her husband. But when she ask Yolanda what happened, Yolanda won't tell her. So I thought about what you told me 'bout them colored whores gettin' beat up and all, and I ask Brenda if this Yolanda's a whore. Brenda, she thinks for a minute, and says could be. At least there be a lot of partyin' goin' on over there and lots of different cars all time of the day and night."

"But she said Yolanda wouldn't say what happened?"

"That's what she say, Doc," Jewel said. "I wish I could tell you more, but that's all I got so far."

"Well, keep at it, would you? The thought of another one of these women coming in like that makes me sick to my stomach."

"Jewel," the doctor said, sipping his coffee, "as long as we're talking, would you mind answering a personal question for me?"

"Depends what it is?"

"What's going on with you and Gabriel White? I know it's none of my business, but you two seem to like each other a lot, and I understand the nature of Gabriel's business, having to travel around all over the place to find work and all, but I was just wondering how come you two haven't settled down together."

"Whoa, Doc," Jewel said, pushing back her chair. "You opened up a big ol' can of worms there fo' sure."

"Well, you don't have to tell me, Jewel, if you don't want to. Like I said, it's none of my business. It's just that, well, this is sort of hard to say, but I really care about you, and I'd like to see you happy, and Gabriel seems to make you happy, and so I was just wondering, being nosy, I guess."

"Well," Jewel said, smoothing the apron on her lap, "it's sort of a long story." She frowned and gazed down at her lap for several seconds. "Gabriel and me go way back," she finally said. "The first time he come through here I fell for him bad. We was both just kids then. But one thing led to another and we was seein' each other every time he come through. Well, my daddy he didn't know nothin' about it. So when I got pregnant, he went crazy. Beat me till I tell him who done it. Then he went searchin' for Gabriel. Finally found him one night playin' at a white club over in Mexico Beach. 'Cause Gabriel can play 'most anything, they had him over there playin' 'Turkey in the Straw' and all kinds of white shit. So Daddy, been drinkin,' comes in there with his shotgun askin' for Gabriel, sayin' he gonna shoot his ass, and this white fellow say hey, what you doin' in here, git outta here fo' I kick yo' black ass. Well, Daddy, he know better, but he's drunk and mightily pissed at Gabriel, so he decks the cracker. He knows right away he's made a big mistake, 'cause there's a bunch of rednecks comin' at him from all directions, but by then it's too late. So he takes them all on, seriously hurtin' a few of them, but manages somehow to get out of there in one piece and back home. Well, as you might have guessed, later that night we get a visit from a carload of fools in white robes and hoods ready to burn our house down and lynch Daddy. Daddy scares 'em off with his shotgun, but he knows they'll be back, so he decides to turn himself into the law rather than have our house torched and him lynched and maybe me and mama hurt in the bargain. The sorry outcome of it all is that Daddy's now servin' ten years of hard labor in Raiford and Gabriel's scared to death that Daddy's gonna kill him when he gets out. So our chance of marryin' is pretty slim. Mama, she loves Gabriel, and Marcus, well, 'course he do, but Daddy, well, I don't know if he'll ever forgive Gabriel. So, you see, Doc, as much as Gabriel and me love each other, we got this little problem with my daddy. He's supposed to git out in a couple of years, but regardless, Gabriel's still a travelin' man and that ain't too good for a marriage either. So I don't know what's gonna happen."

"Oh, Jewel," the doctor said, "I had no idea."

"Doc," Jewel said. "I know you didn't. And I love you as much as my own daddy, bless him, but there's some things you just don't go tellin' a white boss."

"Yes, I understand," the doctor said, "and I appreciate your telling me now, but I, goddammit, don't wanna be just some 'white boss.' I wanna be, oh Christ, Jewel, I don't know what I wanna be, but I'm so sorry that I never asked you about this before."

"That's okay, Doc. I'm sorry too. 'Bout Gabriel, and my daddy, and 'bout you. And, shit, I don't know what to do. Gabriel's for sure gonna end up in New York City on some big radio show, and I'm gonna be here takin' care of you for the rest of my life."

At this point, for the first time ever, the doctor saw Jewel crying. "But, you know what, Doc," she sobbed, "bein' here with you don't sound half bad."

The doctor got up, put his arm around Jewel as she cried. She smelled faintly of laundry soap and lye and felt warm and firm against him.

"Oh hell, Jewel," the doctor said. "I don't know what to say. I don't know what I'd do without you. There's so much I want to say, but I don't know how. I want to say I love you and I want to say I need you and I want you to be happy. And if I could I would, but I don't know what I'm saying."

"Be quiet, Doc."

The doctor held her for a while, and then, when she had stopped crying, he released her and took the dishes from the table and put them in the kitchen sink.

Chapter Twenty-seven

On Wednesday morning, after the doctor had finished all his appointments and was about to go out somewhere for dinner, Nadyne tapped on his office door and told him that he had a telephone call from Sally Martin.

"Good morning," he said. "How are you?"

"Good morning, Van. I'm fine, and I'm so sorry to bother you, but the kids have been hounding me to death about taking you up on your offer to buy them ice cream, and I have to come into town to meet with the people at the Kenney Mill again this afternoon, and I thought if you weren't too busy, I would pick the kids up from school and stop by your office on the way home. Also, I have something that I have to show you."

"What's that?"

"I need to actually show it to you," she said.

"Okay, sounds good. What time should I expect you?"

"Well, I pick up the kids at three, so would three-fifteen work for you?"

"I'll make it work," the doctor said. "See you at three-fifteen here at my office."

The doctor was supposed to be finishing up his house calls at 3:15, but they would just have to wait. Mrs. Porter's chronic rheumatism was not going to be any worse if she had to wait another hour, and he suspected that Jim Eaton's hives would probably have disappeared by the time he got there anyway, regardless of when it was.

He couldn't imagine what Sally wanted to show him, and she didn't do much to assuage his curiosity when she insisted that they go for ice cream before she revealed her secret. After the doctor had given them a tour of the office and they had weighed themselves and measured their heights, except Sally, of course, they all walked over to LeHardy's Pharmacy where they had a fifteen-stool soda fountain and even a few tables. It was another beautiful spring afternoon, and the doctor thought that they must look quite the sight: the aging doctor, the beautiful young widow in her new blue dress, and the four children in their best school clothes marching down Fourth Street to the soda fountain. The doctor insisted that the children each order a sundae of their choice, despite Sally's protestations that so much sugar would ruin their supper. No one could make up their mind on what combination of ice cream and flavored syrup they wanted, but once they got that sorted out, the doctor and Sally left the children at the counter to eat, while they sat at a cafe table nearby and talked.

"So how did it go at the mill?" the doctor asked after a sip of his cherry phosphate.

"Well, I can't believe it, but they offered me a job as a receptionist in the office there. All I have to do is answer the phone and greet people when they come in and type up whatever they need typed. They also want me to set up some sort of filing system, but they're going to teach me how to do that. It doesn't pay a lot, but with the insurance money and the salary we should be able to get by."

"Which mill is it again?" the doctor asked.

"It's called the Kenney Mill. It's on that oak ridge facing the canal right across from the new St. Joe Paper Company. It's brand new. Won't open for another few weeks, so I have time to find someone to look after the kids after school until I get home and hopefully someplace in town to rent so I won't have to drive so far."

"That's great, Sally. Congratulations! I'd love to take you out to supper some night to celebrate properly—I mean with something more than an ice cream sundae."

"That would be fun. I'm hesitant though because it's so soon after Earl's death. If people see us out together they'll surely talk. Even today, in broad daylight, with the kids, I'm sure we'll start some tongues to wagging."

"Well, that's too bad, but I don't care, if you don't," the doctor said. "Maybe if we drove over to the Apalachicola Seafood Grill and had supper no one would notice. I don't think too many folks from Port St. Joe get over there just for supper, so we'd probably be safe. And even if we did get seen, I really don't think it would be that big a deal."

"Well, okay," she said. "Maybe next week sometime. I can't remember the last time that I went out for supper. I'm sure I could get the Winns to keep an eye on the children."

"Just say when."

"Okay, after I show you what I mentioned before, we can decide when."

"So, let me see," the doctor said. "I can't wait."

"Not here. When we get back to the office."

Once there, Sally situated the children in the empty waiting room, reading magazines and doing their homework, and then she and the doctor went back to his office. She dug in her purse until she found an envelope, and from in it she took out a folded piece of plain, white paper and handed it to the doctor. In a small, compact script, it read:

Dearest Sally,

> *I'm sorry to git you involved in this, but I owe a man*
> *sum money. I need you to pay hem so he will not hurt*
> *you and the kids. So please take $2,000 acording to*
> *what he rites below and deliver it to hem. He says he*
> *will hurt you and the kids if you call the police or tell*
> *any one or do not follow what he rites. I'm so sorry for*
> *every thing.*

> *Your loving husband,*
> *Earl*

Written under this in larger block letters was this message:

PUT 100 TWENTY DOLLAR BILLS IN A
SHOE BOX AND PUT IT ON TOP OF THE
FIRST BRICK TOMB AT THE OLD ST.
JOESEPH CEMETARY, BETWEEN 11PM
AND MIDNITE ON FRIDAY, APRIL 15.
COME ALONE.

"This is very strange. This came in the mail? When did you receive it?" the doctor asked.

"Yes, in the mail. Yesterday. It's postmarked Port St. Joe."

"Have you shown it to anyone else?"

"No, not yet, only you. I didn't know what to do."

"Are you afraid?" the doctor asked.

"Yes, I am now. It's so eerie, like Earl coming back from the grave or something. And the part about hurting me and the kids that does scare me."

"It's Earl's handwriting then?"

"Yes, it could be, except for the note at the bottom, of course. The truth is Earl didn't do too much writing."

"Well, it looks like Earl wrote this before he died and gave it to the person he owed money to, to send when he thought the insurance money would be paid."

"Do you think it's this Lucky fellow?" she asked.

"I don't know. I would guess so."

"What should I do?"

"Well, I told the sheriff that I was going to leave this up to him from now on, and I intend to do that."

"But the letter says not to contact the police or tell anyone."

"Well," the doctor said as calmly as he could, "you've already told me, and there is no way I'm going to let you go into a cemetery alone at night with a bunch of money. The sheriff said he thought Lucky would make another move that hopefully would give us a chance to capture him, and it looks like he has. All we have to do is make sure we take advantage of it and get him."

"But what about the children? I don't want anything to happen to them, and this man is clearly crazy."

"Don't worry, we'll take care of them. I'll call the sheriff right now, and we'll figure out how to end this mess once and for all."

"Oh, Van," she said, "let's just pay him and hope he goes away."

"Sally," the doctor said, "people like this don't just go away."

Chapter Twenty-eight

Sheriff Batson, Sally Martin, and the doctor sat around Sally's kitchen table on Thursday afternoon reviewing just how they intended to capture Anthony Lorenzo "Lucky" Lucilla. The doctor had called the sheriff the day before, after Sally and the kids had left, and read him the letter that Sally had brought him. Then this morning the sheriff had called back and asked the doctor to drive out to Sally's house at 4:00 p.m. today, that he had a plan that he would explain to them.

"Okay," the sheriff said, spreading a creased map of Port St. Joe on the kitchen table before them. "Basically, what we're gonna do is surround the cemetery on Friday afternoon. We're gonna use my deputies and Chief Lane's men, since the cemetery is in Port St. Joe and we need all the help we can get. We'll have one man here," the sheriff explained, tapping the map with the tip of his index finger, "right across Garrison Street from the main gate hiding in a dense palmetto and sumac thicket. At night there will be no way to see him. Then we'll have a man on each side of the cemetery hidden behind the thick privet shrub that surrounds the place. Here, here, and here. Again, each will be well hidden and be lying flat on their bellies with a rifle aimed at the first crypt. There are four of these crypts or tombs, each made of brick, that look like large, above-ground coffins. Right about here. I don't know why they're above ground or who's buried in them, but they say most of the graves there are filled with victims of the yellow fever epidemic that wiped out most of the town way back when. That's why some old-timers around here still call it the yellow fever cemetery. Then, on the off chance that our man tries to come in by foot from Twenty-second Street in the back of the cemetery, we'll have a man hiding in one of the houses at the end of the street. Here. He'll be able to see anyone who drives into that dead-end and cuts across the field to the cemetery. The cemetery is not lit at night, and the forecast is for a cloudy and possibly rainy night, so visibility will be poor. But there's no doubt that our men, who will be out there by six o'clock, will have a clear view of everyone who comes or goes. We selected the men who are the best marksmen, so we should have a good chance of stopping him. Chief Lane will be waiting here at Garrison and Twentieth to give chase if he gets that far. If we miss him somehow, I have Pop Albertson on call with his bloodhounds to track him down."

"What about Sally, Mrs. Martin, what is she to do?" the doctor asked.

"Well, unfortunately," the sheriff said, looking at Sally, "we'll need you to get the money as the letter asked and drive to the cemetery tomorrow night between eleven and midnight and put the shoe box on the first tomb. There will be no way he can grab you, because our men will make sure no one comes into the cemetery. So the place will definitely be empty when you get there. Then, after you leave the shoe box, you'll need to get out of there as quickly as possible. Our men will wait until Lucky Lucilla or whoever he is appears to get the money, and then they'll grab him or shoot him, if necessary. To make sure that Mrs. Martin gets to the cemetery without any trouble, I'll follow her in an unmarked car, but at a safe distance so our man doesn't suspect any police involvement. Then after the drop, I'll follow her back home to make sure she returns safe. And I'll be in radio contact with Chief Lane at the cemetery in case Lucky escapes or they need me to help them."

"What about the children?" Sally asked.

"Right, good question," the sheriff said. "That's why I asked you here, Doc. I thought maybe the children would feel safe with you out here, although hopefully they'll all be asleep by the time their mother leaves. And I've asked Harvey to join you with a loaded shotgun. That way if Lucky decides to show up here you can protect the children and hopefully shoot the son of a bitch. But I don't think he'll come here; he'll be more interested in the money. And I know, Doc, I said I wasn't gonna involve you in this anymore, but our forces are spread pretty thin at this point with all those men out at the cemetery, and I don't want to scare the kids with someone they don't know. Harvey could probably handle it by himself, but if something were to happen to him, I'd feel more comfortable with a backup. Like I said, I don't expect he'll come out here, but just to be on the safe side. Any questions?"

"Why do we have to bring real money if we know we're going to catch him?" Sally asked.

"Well," the sheriff answered. "I thought about that and figured if somehow he did grab the shoe box and get away and found that it didn't have real money in it, then, being the nut that he is, he might come lookin' for you and the children. I figure your safety is more important than the money. So it's sort of an insurance policy in case something goes wrong and we don't capture him. My guess is if he gets the money he'll be long gone. That's apparently the reason he's been sticking around so long."

"What if this man sees one of your men or suspects something fishy is going on, that he's been set up?" the doctor asked.

"I'm afraid," the sheriff said, "that, that's a chance we'll have to take.

If we scare him off, he'll be back, sooner or later, and, until then, we'll have the Martin house and the kids protected by an officer around the clock. Okay? Then I'll count on you getting the money, Mrs. Martin, and putting it in a shoe box, and, Doc, I'll see you back here tomorrow night at ten o'clock."

The next night, Good Friday, as it turned out, the doctor was back at the appointed time, where he found Harvey Winn, sitting in a rocking chair, this time on Sally Martin's front porch, smoking his pipe, as usual, but with a double-barrel, twelve-gauge shotgun at his side. When the sheriff arrived in a few minutes, looking tired and nervous, he reviewed the plan with everyone, twice, and then, checking his watch, walked to his unmarked car, a late model Chevy Master. Sally took the Buster Brown shoe box that she had borrowed from Ronald, gave the doctor's hand a private squeeze, and hurried to her car. The doctor and Harvey sat on the front porch listening to the sound of the cars recede inland as the waves lapped gently on the shore and a silent mist began to fall.

"How are your retirement plans coming?" the doctor asked, as a waft of Prince Edward tobacco smoke blew his way.

"Actually very good. I found a job as a night watchman at the new paper mill and I start May first. I already told the service that I was done, so they're looking for a replacement now, for both Earl and me."

"So you'll be moving into town then?"

"Yep, soon as I find a place."

Harvey and the doctor continued to talk about the keeper's new life and some of his memories of his old. The man was definitely sad about leaving his quiet life on the beach, but he knew it was time, and his wife and children were thrilled. The fact was the lighthouse keeper himself had fallen under the spell of the lighthouse's spooky aura.

"Five years is enough," the keeper said. "Too many bad things happen here, too much isolation. The truth is Mary, my wife, she's the jealous type, thinks I have a thing for Sally Martin. Could be she's right. I do like the woman, but ain't nothin' ever happened between us. But the wife would just as soon see us be as far apart as possible. Now, as it turns out, both Sally and her family and me and mine are movin' into town. But it'll be different there. We won't be all alone like we are out here. Hopefully, for my wife's sake, we'll find places at the opposite ends of town. At any rate, it's time to move on. But just between you and me, I'll miss her though, Sally. Seein' her everyday has been a sheer delight."

Before the doctor could figure out how to respond to Harvey's confession, they heard a car approaching. Harvey jumped up and grabbed his shotgun, and the doctor stood at attention in front of the door. The car was moving faster than was safe down the narrow road through the steady drizzle. The children were upstairs asleep, he hoped. As the approaching car skidded past the head lighthouse keeper's cottage, the keeper himself raised the shotgun to his shoulder and took aim at the car's rain-splattered windshield. It looked like Harvey was about to pull the trigger when the car slid to a stop inches in front of the Martin's front porch stairs. Then, the car door flew open and there was a sobbing Sally Martin, running through the rain toward them. She ran directly to the doctor's arms, as Harvey lowered his shotgun.

"What's wrong?" the doctor asked. "What happened? Are you all right? Come inside. I'll make you a cup of tea."

The three of them went to the kitchen, and the doctor lit the burner under the tea kettle as Sally collapsed in a chair at the table and shivered. The doctor took off his suit coat and wrapped it around her trembling shoulders.

"It was awful," she sobbed. "I was driving down the road from here, and when I got almost to Cape San Blas Road, a tall pine fell right in front of my car. It almost hit me. I had to stop the car because it was blocking the road. And as soon as I did, the passenger door opened and a man grabbed the shoe box and was gone just like that. By the time the sheriff got there, he'd disappeared into the woods."

"Are you okay?" the doctor asked.

"I think so. It happened so fast. The sheriff took out after him in the woods, but he was gone. It was too dark to see anything. So the sheriff told me to come back here while he radioed the chief and the other men and got Pop Albertson and his dogs out here."

"Did you get a look at him?" Harvey asked.

"Just barely," Sally said. "He was in and out before I knew it. But he did look kinda tall, and he had curly hair, and he was sort of dark, but everything was dark out there, and it happened so fast, I couldn't be sure."

The doctor handed her a cup of tea and put his arm around her, and Harvey excused himself to go check on the light.

"Now what?" she murmured as the doctor held her.

"I don't know," the doctor said. "I guess we wait."

"For what?'

"For all this to be over," the doctor answered. "For this Lucky man to go away. For life to get back to normal. For you and the kids to move into town where you'll be closer to me. Maybe . . . maybe for us to be together?"

"That's a lot of waiting," she said, looking up at the doctor.

"I know. But I don't know what else to do."

So they waited there and drank more tea and talked about the children and how each was different and how much Sally loved them. And they talked about Sally's new job and how afraid she was, since she had never worked in a real job before. And what life would be like in town with so many people nearby. And, as they listened to Pop Albertson's bloodhounds baying in the distance, the doctor told her about how it was when he first moved to Port St. Joe and how insular the people were at first until he got to know them. And then, before they knew it, it was morning and the sky had cleared and the sun was coming up, and a sheriff's deputy drove up in front of the house and told the doctor that he could go home now, that he was there to watch the house and drive the kids to school until they caught Lucky Lucilla, who was apparently still loose out there somewhere with a Buster Brown shoe box full of Sally Martin's money.

Chapter Twenty-nine

The doctor slept most of the next day since it was Saturday and he did not have to go to the office. Sometime in the late afternoon, a loud thunderclap woke him from a terrible nightmare in which he was treating Jewel, who had been beaten up by someone she would not identify. The doctor was sweating and angry when he finally got out of bed and took a long, hot shower. He had finished *Of Mice and Men* a few days before, and he was still ruminating about the comradeship of men—Gator and him, Gabriel and Reggie—and the seductiveness of some women—Sally?—and wondering again exactly what he was getting himself into. Still in his robe, he was just starting *Their Eyes Were Watching God* when the phone rang, and he found Jewel on the line asking in a hoarse whisper if she and Gabriel could come over for a minute. Of course, he told her, wondering what they could possibly be up to on a Saturday evening before Easter Sunday.

Both Jewel and Gabriel were soaked from the rain which was now blowing in hard from the west and in a state of agitation when they arrived and sat with the doctor around the kitchen table.

"Okay, what's the matter?" he asked, as he handed them both a towel to dry off with.

"Reggie," Jewel began, "you remember, Gabriel's friend who was playin' all those instruments with Gabriel on your birthday?"

"Yeah, of course," the doctor said, "I remember him. What about him?"

"He's gone plum crazy," Gabriel said as he leaned back in his chair to shake off his wet cap over the kitchen sink behind him. Said he seen somethin' he wasn't s'posed to see and he's afraid he's gonna git killed if he doesn't git outta here fast."

"What could he have possibly seen?" the doctor asked.

"Let me tell you what he said," Gabriel said. "We ain't workin this weekend, it bein' Good Friday and Easter and all, nobody hirin', so I was havin' supper with Jewel last night and Reggie, he decided to go fishin' over at Lighthouse Bayou, s'posed to be some redfish bitin' over there a fellow tell him. So that's the last I seen of him, headin' out to Lighthouse Bayou. But he never come back last night to the little shack we rentin'. He didn't show up till just a little while ago wantin' to pack and git outta there fast. Said he'd been hidin' out and now he was movin' on. So I told him to wait just a minute while I got Jewel, maybe she could help. So he said okay, but just a minute."

"So when I got there, he's all packed and ready to go," Jewel said. "The boy's wound up like a cheap alarm clock. I asked him what happened, and he hemmed and hawed around and finally tell us he seen a white man dump a body in the bayou while he was fishin' from the shore, and, after he dump the body, this white man seen Reggie, so Reggie, he took off."

"Well, why's he so afraid? We'll just go to the sheriff and Reggie can tell him what happened and the sheriff can handle it."

"We told him that," Jewel said. "We told him that just 'cause he seen somethin' he wasn't s'posed to see doesn't mean he's in trouble. But he says no, he says that he believes this white man will somehow turn it around on Reggie, and Reggie, he'll git the blame for killin' the guy who got dumped in the ocean. He's mighty shook up 'bout it. Shakin' like a fifty-cent ladder. Just knows he's gonna go to jail for somethin' he had nothin' to do with."

"Well, I don't exactly understand what he's so afraid of," the doctor said. "But then again I'm white and well off, and he's not. So is he gone then?"

"No, not yet," Gabriel said. "At least, I hope not. It took us some time, but we finally convinced him to talk to you before he left. Jewel promised him that he could trust you and that you could maybe git the whole story from him and then make sure he didn't git blamed for it. He said that the only way he figured he could git outta this mess was that a white man believed him, 'cause he say he know he just be in big trouble with the law if he tell them what he seen."

"Well," the doctor said, "I'll be happy to talk to him. I'm not sure what good it's gonna do, but I'll do my best. Just let me finish dressing and I'll drive over there. Meanwhile, you guys better get back there and make sure Reggie doesn't take off. Now, tell me where he's at."

"Up in the colored section," Jewel said. "In North Port St. Joe, past my house, out at the far end of Peters Street, next to the tracks."

"I'll find it," the doctor said, although it had been some time since he had been in that part of town, since most Negroes hesitated to ask him to make house calls because they knew they couldn't afford to pay for them.

After Jewel and Gabriel had left the doctor's house, he called Sheriff Batson in Wewahitchka and was surprised to find him still in his office on a stormy Saturday night. "Yeah, I'm still here," the sheriff said. "Still hopin' that something will turn up on this Lucky Lucilla man. Pop's dogs couldn't find a thing, 'cept a raccoon they ran up a tree and barked at for about an hour. So I got everybody out lookin', but my bet is the man's gone. He's got what he wanted, the money, so there's no reason for him to hang around now. So I've called the state police and asked them to put out an all-points on him, and we'll see what turns up. Meanwhile, I'll have a man keep an eye on the Martins for a few days just to make sure. What's up with you?"

The doctor explained what Gabriel and Jewel had reported, but he admitted that the details were so sketchy at this point that he didn't know what, if anything, was really going on. He told the sheriff that he was going to drive over to see Reggie at his place at the end of Peters Street and if anything came of it, he would call the sheriff and let him know and try to get Reggie to talk to him.

"Well, I'd feel more comfortable if you'd let me talk to the man," the sheriff said, "after what you been through. I can be over there in a few minutes."

"That's okay, Sheriff, I think I'll be safe there with Jewel and Gabriel around. And it's probably all just some kind of misunderstanding anyway. This man Reggie seems harmless enough, and he said he didn't want the law involved, for some reason, so he would probably hightail it if you showed up. And besides I guess I kind of promised Jewel and Gabriel that I'd come alone. So we'll see what happens. Sounds like you got your hands full there anyway. I'll check it out and give you a call back in the morning. I'm sure it's nothing."

"Are you sure, Doc?" the sheriff said, as the wind and the rain outside picked up, causing the phone connection to become suddenly scratchy. "I don't know anything about this Reggie character, but if you say he's harmless, I guess I'll take your word for it. But I'd feel a lot better if you'd let me talk to him."

"What was that?" the doctor asked through the static.

"Be careful."

Chapter Thirty

As the storm that had been brewing all afternoon now grew in intensity, the doctor drove through the driving rain, bounced over the bumpy Apalachicola Northern Railroad tracks that divided the town between north and south, black and white, to the end of the rutted, muddy road that he thought was Peters Street. There, he found a single, little nondescript shack, but it was totally dark. The entire street was dark, in fact, with no streetlights and only a few lights on in the houses farther down the road toward the intersection of Avenue F. Had the doctor misunderstood which street he was supposed to go to? He parked his car in front of the unpainted clapboard shack that was the only one at the end of Peters. This had to be the one, but there was no sign of life anywhere. Maybe he was too late. Maybe Reggie had thought better of talking to the doctor and took off for parts unknown. Well, the doctor thought, he had come this far, he might as well knock on the door to see if anybody was there. With his raincoat flapping in the wind and his shoes covered with mud, the doctor knocked several times and was about to leave when a small, muffled voice came from inside.

"Who is it?"

"Dr. Berber. Is that you, Reggie?"

"Yes, are you alone?"

"Yes," the doctor said. "I'm alone."

"Okay. Just a minute, I'll unlock it."

The doctor heard a chain rattling inside and finally the windowless door opened and there stood little Reggie in a black T-shirt and overalls, shivering and looking scared.

"There's a chair over there," Reggie said.

"That's okay, I'll stand. Where're Jewel and Gabriel? And how come there're no lights on in here?"

"I sent them away. I told Jewel and Gabriel that I didn't want them involved in this. If they know too much they might be in trouble like I am, so I sent them away and promised them that I would wait here until you got here. You sure you're alone. I thought I heard something else out there."

"No, I'm alone," the doctor assured him. "No one's here except you and me. So what's this all about? And could you light that lantern over there? I can't see a damn thing."

Reggie took a match from the box on the table in the corner and, his hands shaking nervously, finally lit the kerosene lantern. It didn't put out much light, but at least the doctor could see Reggie's frightened face and the contents of the single room that was apparently home to the traveling troubadours while they were in town: a square wooden table in the corner with three rickety chairs around it and the lantern on top of it; a wood-burning stove in the opposite corner; two unmade cots on opposite walls, on one of which rested Reggie's packed valise; a tall chiffonier next to a single open, unscreened window; and an antique icebox near the back door.

"Well, Reggie let's hear it. What happened that's got you so scared?"

As the wind and some rain blew through the open window, Reggie looked around as if to make sure the doctor hadn't sneaked someone else into the little room and said, "Last night I was fishin' from the bank at Lighthouse Bayou. It must have been after midnight. I had a little canvas lean-to set up to keep the drizzle off of me and was drinkin' a little whiskey and I must've fallen asleep. Anyway, I'm still layin' there and I wake up and I see a motorboat out in the bayou. There's a man in it, and he's out there maybe fifty yards or so, and then he cuts the motor and he pulls a body out of the bottom of the boat and he pushes it over the side into the water. Damn near tipped over the boat. Then he starts the engine up again and looks like he's comin' straight at me. I don't know what to do, so I freezed, too afraid to do anything else. Then, 'fore I know it, he's right on top of me. Not much farther than from me to you. And that's when I seen who he was. Well, I took off runnin' and he shot his gun at me, but he missed, and I got back to my car as fast as I could and I got outta there fast. I spent the whole day hid out in the woods tryin' to figure out what to do. Finally, figured the only thing to do was to come back here, git my stuff, and git outta town as fast as I could. Then Gabriel and Jewel come and tried to talk me out of it, but I don't see no other way."

"Who was the man who dumped the body, Reggie, that's making you so afraid?"

Reggie didn't answer. The rain was now beating fiercely against the house's tin roof and the thunder was rumbling closer and closer.

"Who was it, Reggie?" the doctor asked again. "I'm here to help you, not get you in trouble."

"It was the sheriff," Reggie said finally. "He had on a big ol' shiny star right there on his gray shirt. Plain as day."

Suddenly, as thunder cracked overhead and a bolt of lightning brightened the room, the front door flew open and Sheriff Batson stood before them with his gun drawn. Reggie dove toward the open window, and, just as the sheriff aimed and was about to fire into his back, Gator Mica burst through the open front door and knocked the gun out of the sheriff's hand. Reggie was out the window and gone into the night. The sheriff was scrambling for his gun that had slid across the floor while Gator tried to stop him by jumping on his back and dragging him down. The doctor tried to ease around them as they wrestled on the floor to get to the gun, but the sheriff had elbowed Gator in the ribs and was now on top of him pummeling his face with his fists, blocking his way. Gator finally managed to raise a knee and smash it between the sheriff's legs, causing the sheriff to roll off Gator but right on top of the gun just as the doctor was reaching for it. As both the doctor and Gator dove for the gun, the sheriff rolled away with it in his hand. "Back off," the sheriff panted, as he scooted on the seat of his pants against the back door, the gun in front of him in two outstretched hands, "or I'll blow your brains out."

The doctor and Gator did as they were told, as the sheriff slowly stood up, the gun still aimed at them. "I wondered what took you so long," the sheriff snorted. "You had to go pick up your Injun friend on the way, I see."

"Sorry, Sheriff," the doctor said. "It was a little out of the way, but I thought I might need the company, even if he was on the floorboards in the back."

"Well," the sheriff said, "it looks like I'm the only company you're going to get tonight. Both of you, slowly now, back up against that wall behind you. Any fast moves and I'll shoot you."

"Do you mind telling us what this is all about?" the doctor asked as he shuffled backwards. "Whose body were you dumping out there in Lighthouse Bayou?"

"I'm not sure that's any of your business, Doc, under the circumstances. Instead, I'm gonna ask you a question. Why shouldn't I kill you right now?"

"Well, for one, Sheriff," the doctor answered. "You'd have a lot of explaining to do, since I also stopped by Chief Lane's office on my way and told him that Gator and I were coming out here and that you knew about it."

"Okay," the sheriff said. "I could probably explain my way out of that some way, but you're probably right. It would be messy and I'd have a lot of lying to do. So what happens then if I let you go?"

"We go to Chief Lane and Judge Denton and we tell them what happened last night."

"And what exactly was that?"

"That you were seen dumping a body into Lighthouse Bayou."

"And whose body might that be, Doc?"

"I don't know. You tell me."

"What if I told you that I shot Lucky Lucilla as he was trying to escape with Sally Martin's money?"

"Okay," the doctor said. "But why in the world would you want to dump him into the ocean in the middle of the night? You'd be a hero, after all, if you brought him in, dead or alive."

"Well, let's put it this way. The sheriff in Franklin County and all these G-men aren't the only ones who benefit from Dr. Price's generosity. If I brought Lucky Lucilla in alive, he might, in exchange for leniency, be tempted to tell more than he should about Dr. Price's business, and, if I brought him in dead, then we'd have a body on our hands that someone might connect to Dr. Price and, as you know, the good doctor likes to keep a low profile. It's just cleaner this way. Lucky Lucilla disappears and the whole episode blows over. End of story."

"But I still don't understand," the doctor said, "why Lucky killed Martin, if, in fact he did. If Martin was going to get this loan that his uncle arranged, then why did he murder him?"

"Well, that's the same question I asked Lucky before I dumped him into the bay. And what he told me was that Martin and him had become close, like brothers, he said, and so one night he had told Martin about how he had killed his family. And at about this time, Martin was getting deeper and deeper into debt and having trouble at home, so he hatched this plan where he would up his life insurance so that when he died his wife could pay off all his debts and he could somehow feel better about all the grief he had put her through. And so he hired his so-called friend Lucky Lucilla to kill him and wrote this letter to his wife and gave it to Lucky. But when Martin told Lucky that the deal was off, that his uncle had arranged a loan that would get him out of debt, Lucky said he went crazy. He couldn't believe that someone he considered to be his brother would renege on a deal and not pay him what he had promised, so he apparently became enraged and killed Martin anyway."

"That's some story," Gator said, standing there against the wall next to the doctor.

"Isn't it though?" the sheriff said with his gun still aimed at the pair. "So, here's the deal, as I see it. I can shoot you now, or I can let you go. We've already been through the messiness of shooting you. So if I let you go, you could always kill me, but, Doc, I don't think you have the stomach for that, the Hippocritical Oath, or whatever it's called, and hopefully you could control your friend Gator here so he wouldn't do anything that stupid. So if I let you go and if you wouldn't kill me, then what's to keep you from going to Chief Lane or Judge Denton, as you suggest, Doc?"

"Nothing that I can think of," the doctor answered.

"Well, let me see what I can think of. Let's say you went to Lane or Denton or somebody else, it would then be your word against mine, right? I doubt we'll ever see your friend Reggie again and apparently he didn't tell anyone who he saw except you two. I just happened to be out searching for Lucky Lucilla all last night and didn't go any place near

Lighthouse Bayou and neither did you. And if you, Gator, was to say anything to these fellows, I guess I'd have no choice but to tell them about the warrant that's still outstanding for your arrest for killing a man in a bar in Florida City a few years back. And if you, Doc, was to say something, I guess I'd have to bring up the circumstances of your leaving Lynn Haven City before you came here, how the word got around town about your nasty little morphine habit. Amazing what someone in my position can find out when he asks. Found that out when I checked on Lucky Lucilla with the state. And then, of course, the whole issue of the widow Martin's life insurance payment. If our little friend Stanton was to find out that Lucky was actually hired by Martin to do him in, then I suspect the insurance company would want the money back that they've already paid. So what's to tell, really? Mrs. Martin gets what she deserves after living with a rotten husband all those years. Lucky Lucilla gets what he deserves for killing his family and murdering his best friend for a lousy two grand. And for y'all and me, we get what we may or may not deserve. But, at any rate, life goes on. Business as usual. What do you think? Do you buy it or do I shoot you now?"

The doctor thought for a moment that maybe this would be a good way to end it all: let the sheriff do the deed. But instead he just looked at Gator. Gator looked at the doctor. They both shrugged, and the sheriff lowered his gun.

Chapter Thirty-one

The storm began to subside as the doctor and Gator drove away from the little shack at the end of Peters Street. They were trying to find Jewel's house a few blocks over on Avenue C. The trouble was there were no street signs or street lamps in this part of town, but somehow the doctor remembered that the other end of Peters Street was at Avenue C. So he drove back down the street and then guessed that he should take a right on what he hoped was Avenue C.

The last time he was in North Port St. Joe was last summer when Jewel's old Ford had broken down and he had taken her home. The little shanty town, called "Nigger Town" by most white people, was a hodgepodge of narrow dirt streets and ramshackle shotgun shacks. People were out in their yards, barbecuing over halved oil drums, and listening or dancing to blues music on their radios. With Jewel beside him in the front seat, they were greeted by waves and smiles as they drove down Jewel's street, hailed as if they were some sort of prodigal sons. The doctor knew and had treated many of the people he saw out in their yards at a time when most white hospitals and doctors in the South would not see

Negro patients at all.

But tonight Avenue C was a dark, slippery quagmire, and the doctor and Gator could not tell one unpainted shotgun shack from another. They tried to locate Jewel's car, but there seemed to be a lot of old, black Fords parked on the street, none particularly recognizable as Jewel's. Like most good sons of the South, Gator and the doctor were loath to stop and ask anyone for directions. There weren't any people outside anyway at this hour on a rainy Easter Eve night, so it would be an additional indignity to actually knock on a stranger's door. As a result, they drove aimlessly up and down Avenue C for a while, hoping for a sign, of what kind, they were both uncertain. The doctor was about to give up and go back to his own house and call Jewel on the telephone, when the sign, in the form of Gabriel White, appeared on the front porch of a house near Battles Street. When Gabriel spotted them, he waved them over and invited them inside.

As they stepped out of the car into the mud, a skinny mongrel dog stuck his nose out from under the house's sagging porch and began yapping incessantly until Gabriel shushed him and opened the front door for them to enter. The bedraggled pair wiped their muddy shoes on the straw mat and followed Gabriel in. There they found the typical shotgun shack design: one long hall down the middle, with doors on each side, leading off into narrow side rooms, which Jewel had shown him last summer. Off to the right side of the hallway, if the doctor remembered correctly, were three small bedrooms, one for Jewel, another for Marcus, and the last for Jewel's mother. And on the left were a kitchen in the rear, next to a dining room, and then a parlor in front, into which Gabriel now led Gator and the doctor. The place smelled like supper, which had been pinto beans and ham hocks, if the doctor's nose was not deceiving him. The parlor was small and furnished simply with an old maroon felt couch, a rocking chair, and a low coffee table with an open Bible lying on it. Theirs was obviously not an affluent existence, but, owing to Jewel's and her mother's hard work, they were better off than most of their neighbors. Jewel's mother tended a vegetable garden in the backyard and also took in laundry and ironing from a few white families, as well as doing most of the cooking and housekeeping for the three of them.

"Jewel," Gabriel yelled, "look what the cat dragged in. Well, really, who I found out driving up and down in front of your house.

"Oops, I better hold it down. Marcus and Jewel's mama are already asleep in the back. You want a drink?"

"I think maybe I could use one," Gator said.

"Yeah, me too, thanks," the doctor said.

"Be right back."

Then Jewel appeared, drying her hands on a dish towel and pointing at the old maroon couch for Gator and the doctor to sit on. They faced a white wall with three framed pictures on it: one of a young Jewel in her high school graduation gown, one of a middle-aged Negro man in a dark suit, who the doctor assumed was Jewel's father, and one, in the center, of a long-haired, bearded white Jesus. Jewel sat down on the edge of the rocking chair and Gabriel returned with two jelly glasses full of moonshine for the doctor and Gator.

"So what happened?" Jewel prompted. "Where's Reggie? He sent us away. Who did he see last night? What are you doing here, Gator?"

The doctor, with Gator's help, laid out the entire story—who Reggie had seen, the sheriff's surprise appearance, his struggle with Gator, and what Lucky Lucilla had told the sheriff, and why the sheriff had killed him—everything except the part about Gator's arrest warrant in Florida City and the details of the doctor's move from Lynn Haven City.

"So the insurance investigator and I were right," Jewel said. "There was something fishy going on all along. And that Martin rascal wasn't such a bad guy after all. At least his family can get out of debt now and get on with their lives."

"As long as we all keep our mouths shut," Gator said. Everyone was quiet for a moment, contemplating the implications of Gator's pronouncement. Finally the doctor leaned over and said, "Gabriel, I'm so sorry I called the sheriff and let Reggie get away. I just had no idea. I thought if Reggie was in any real danger that I'd have Gator come along, but it turns out that the real danger was from the sheriff himself."

"Oh, don't think a thing about it, Doc," Gabriel said. "I know where to find Reggie. We've been friends since we was kids, and he ain't got but one or two places where he goes to hide. I'll find him, don't you worry. But I doubt you'll be seein' him back in this town anytime soon, not as long as that sheriff's still alive anyway."

"Well, that's too bad," the doctor said, "but I guess it's the way it has to be. I don't think the sheriff would be too happy to see Reggie again either."

"Well, I guess that's it then," Jewel said, looking around one by one to each of them in the dim little parlor. "The murderer is dead and the Martins get to keep the insurance money."

"Happy Easter," the doctor said, as he and Gator downed their drinks, stood up, and headed home.

Chapter Thirty-two

As the doctor was driving Gator back to his secluded, makeshift house in the dunes, Gator hatched the idea of stopping by the Indian Pass Raw Bar for something to eat since it was on the way and probably the only place around Port St. Joe that was open this late on Easter Eve. It was well past 10:00 p.m., and they were both starving, and the doctor was too worn out to worry about whether Lucky Lucilla was really dead or whether there might be someone else waiting there to attack him with an oyster rake again. The place was still open and looked busy when they found a parking spot near the road and joined the crowd inside. The old lady who owned the roadhouse, Sadie McIntire, was still at her cash register near the front door, but she was too busy to notice them as they found a couple of open stools at the bar. Jimmie Davis was singing "Meet Me Tonight in Dreamland" on the juke box and the place was even noisier and smokier than the doctor remembered it. They each ordered a Spearman beer, a dozen local Lagoon oysters, a bowl of gumbo, and a piece of key lime pie.

"Well, partner," Gator said, as he squeezed lemon juice on an oyster,

"I guess we got in over our heads on this one, but at least it's all over. As the sheriff said, we can all go back to business as usual now."

"Yeah, in a way, I guess the sheriff is right. It's best for Sally Martin if none of this comes out. She gets to keep the money. And this guy Lucky got what he deserved."

"Yeah, and we all get to keep our little secrets too. You and me, and the sheriff too," Gator said as he downed another oyster. "We even get to keep enjoyin' our favorite moonshine. What could be better for all concerned?"

"So why is it then," the doctor said, "that I feel so lousy?"

"Don't know, partner. Could be a lot worse."

"Yeah, I guess so," the doctor said.

They each had a cup of coffee with their pie, and then the doctor drove Gator the rest of the way home. The roads to Gator's camp were muddy, but the rain had stopped and the stars were beginning to shine through around the few remaining clouds. Their world smelled like a soggy swamp. Yes, the doctor thought, it could be worse, but he still felt dissatisfied and couldn't help but wish that it had all ended up differently somehow.

He consoled himself by considering Sally Martin. The sheriff's solution was certainly the best for her and her family, and the sheriff was right—they, if anybody, deserved the money and the possibility of a new life. So, the doctor thought, he would take the next step in seeing if he could somehow make himself a part of that life.

He called her on Monday morning and didn't say a word about his Saturday rendezvous with the sheriff, but he did remind her that they had most certainly seen the last of Lucky Lucilla since he had her money and was probably in another state by now. She agreed, even though she had just watched her children climb into a sheriff deputy's car to take them to school. She said that she felt more secure now that she had had a chance to settle down from Friday night's encounter. The sheriff was planning to remove his deputy from watching her house if nothing further occurred in the next few days, and she thought it would be fine if the doctor came out for supper on this coming Friday night, but she didn't feel comfortable leaving the children to have supper with him in Apalachicola just yet.

The next morning at breakfast Jewel again asked if she could join the doctor. "Of course," he said. "Anytime, don't bother to ask. Just sit down. What's on your mind?"

"Well, remember we was talkin' the other mornin' 'bout Gabriel and me, and how he's maybe gonna git on the radio someday and move to New York. Well, it looks like the day's come. Gabriel got a letter yesterday askin' him to come on up there and talk with this man Huey about a contract and start doin' some rehearsin' for the show."

"That's great, Jewel. But what about you?"

"Well, Gabriel says the man only sent him enough money for him to go up there, so he's goin' by hisself, but, if everything goes okay, he'll send for me and Marcus to come join him."

"And you intend to do that?" the doctor asked, as he peered into Jewel's pretty brown eyes.

"Well, despite what we was talkin' about the other day 'bout me spendin' the rest of my days here in Port St. Joe takin' care of you, I do love that man, and if he wants me, I'd go."

"I understand, Jewel, and I don't blame you a bit. You'd be stupid to stay here with me if Gabriel's up in New York getting rich singing on the radio."

"Well, that remains to be seen. And I'll believe it when I see it if he calls me to come up there with him. So, my guess is you're stuck with me longer than you think."

"God, I hope so, Jewel."

"You want some more grits?"

"No, thanks," the doctor said, "but as long as we're confessing here I might as well tell you about Sally Martin, the widow of the man who was murdered out there at the Cape San Blas Lighthouse. I've been seeing her a few times since then, and we've sort of become friends."

"Friends?" Jewel said.

"Yes, friends."

"What kinda friends?"

"Just friends."

"Then how come you blushin', Doc? I been wonderin' when you was gonna tell me 'bout that. You been hangin' 'round out there like a hound dog with a bone. So let's hear it."

The doctor told her about Sally Martin, how beautiful and down to earth she was, and about their times together and what a good cook she was, and how much he enjoyed being with her and her kids and how he hoped that something more would come of it all.

"Like marriage, you mean?" Jewel asked.

"I don't know, Jewel. I haven't got that far yet. Like something. Like being together more maybe, now that they're moving into town."

"Well, Doc, you know I wish you well, but I just want y'all to think about how this woman might be what my mama calls 'griefin' needy,' not to mention what people gonna say with her husband not yet cold in his grave, and your age differences—why you must be twice her age—and the kids, Doc, you ain't never had no kids. You sure you know what you gittin' into?"

"No, Jewel, I don't. But don't think I haven't thought about all those things. I know I run a big risk of looking foolish here, but for some reason I don't care that much anymore. I like her, she likes me. I'm gonna see where it goes, regardless of what you or other people think."

"Good for you, Doc. That's what I was hopin' you would say. God knows you both deserve to be happy, and you got my blessin', for what it's worth, to do whatever you gotta do. I hope she makes you happy as a clam at high tide."

"Thanks, Jewel, I appreciate that, although, to tell you the truth, I'm more than a little concerned about this Gabriel thing. On the one hand, I would hate like hell to see you go, but, on the other, I want you to be happy too. So I guess what I'm trying to say is that I want you to do what you have to do too."

"Thanks, Doc. We'll see what happens."

"Meanwhile, why don't we give Gabriel a send-off? When's he leaving?"

"Second week of May is the plan."

"How about the Sunday before he leaves then? I know he'll be working Friday and Saturday nights and you two will want some time alone together, I'm sure, so we'll make it an early night."

"Sounds great, Doc," Jewel said. "You're a sweetheart, you know it?"

"Yeah, well, we'll see about that."

Chapter Thirty-three

The following few weeks passed without major incident. The doctor continued seeing patients, as usual, as well as Sally Martin who was planning to start her new job at the Kenney Mill when it opened on May 16. She had located a house in town, on Sixth Street, a few blocks away from the doctor's house, but it wasn't available for her to move into until June 1. Harvey Winn, the jittery lighthouse keeper, had started his job as a night watchman at the big new St. Joe Paper Company mill, but had not yet found a place on the other side of town from Sally Martin to move to. Gabriel White continued to play his music around the area, polishing his repertoire for his upcoming radio debut in New York City, without Reggie, of course, who had not been heard from since the night he had dived out the window of the shack at the end of Peters Street and disappeared into the night.

The tupelo honey season was now in full bloom in Wewahitchka, with beekeepers from all over the South descending upon the little town to take advantage of the brief two-week harvesting period when the tupelo gum tree blossomed along the swampy edges of the Chipola and Apalachicola River basin. Presumably, this annual event was keeping Sheriff Batson busy, because the doctor had not seen or heard from him since their revealing encounter on Easter weekend.

Anthony Lorenzo "Lucky" Lucilla's body was never recovered from St. Joseph Bay where the sheriff had dumped it, but, much to the doctor's distress, the body of a Negro prostitute was. His worst fear regarding the escalating violence against these women was now realized, and he vowed once again to find some way to put a stop to it. Unfortunately, Jewel's information pipeline had not produced one viable lead so far, and Jewel, for whatever reason, seemed more morose with each passing day.

Gator Mica was also making himself scarce, and the doctor wondered if he was all right. The fact that Gator had killed a man in a bar fight in Florida City, as the sheriff reported, did not surprise the doctor. He remembered Gator telling him that he had to leave town fast because of an altercation he had with a past lover's new boyfriend. Gator had just not given him all the details, that's all.

Likewise, the doctor had not given anyone in Port St. Joe, including Gator, the particulars of his departure from Lynn Haven City three years before. He was disturbed that the sheriff had found out, but apparently there was some official record that he was able to access that divulged at least some of the circumstances of his leaving for Port St. Joe back then. After Carrie Jo had died in 1933, the doctor had fallen into another deep depression similar to the one he had experienced after Annie had vanished. He consumed more morphine, and he avoided everyone except his patients. Without Carrie Jo as his nurse, his practice soon became a disaster. He couldn't juggle all the appointments like she could, and he couldn't keep track of the billing and necessary payments.

He would have simply closed up shop if it hadn't been for Jennie Langdon. At first, she was his patient. He had cured her monthly migraine headaches by advising her to drink peppermint tea with tupelo honey whenever she felt them coming on. And, in gratitude and probably pity, she had offered to help him out in the office, which by then was clearly being mismanaged and descending quickly into complete disarray. Although she was not a nurse, she knew how to do everything else that needed to be done to make his practice viable, from cleaning, to filing, to billing, to calling a plumber when the toilet backed up; she handled it all with aplomb. And, in gratitude for her help and enchanted by her dark-eyed beauty, he fell for her. They were married in the spring and by fall they knew why people had advised them not to be in such a hurry. The doctor, more out of habit than ill will, treated her like a subordinate at home, and Jennie rightfully expected something more egalitarian. She assumed their romantic courtship would continue after they were married, and the doctor preferred to settle into a more relaxed domestic routine like he had with Annie and Carrie Jo. The doctor hid his morphine habit from Jennie, and, then when she discovered it, she demanded that he stop and accused him of lying by not telling her about it before they were married. But, try as he might, the doctor could not break either habit, neither the morphine nor the domestic stagnation, so all too quickly the marriage and the office relationship faltered. And Jennie, more out of frustration than antagonism, spread the word around the small town about the doctor's morphine addiction. It was her way of letting her friends and family know that it was not her fault, but the doctor's, that their marriage had failed so precipitously.

Without Jennie in the office and without the respect of the community, the doctor's practice soon degenerated. And when a new doctor arrived in town, and Dr. Berber found out that Port St. Joe was looking for a doctor, he decided it was time to make a move. So he closed his practice in Lynn Haven City and moved the thirty-six miles to Port St. Joe, where he was fortunate enough to find Nadyne and Jewel, who made it possible for him to continue practicing medicine. How much of this the sheriff knew about, the doctor had no idea, but he would just as soon forget about it and not have anything about his morphine addiction known among the good people of Port St. Joe.

The doctor knew that if he were contemplating marriage with Sally Martin that he should not make the same mistake that he had with Jennie and hide his drug habit, but he didn't know just how to bring it up, and he was still uncertain that their relationship was in fact leading to matrimony.

On the clear evening of Friday, May 6th, the doctor again visited Sally Martin and her family on Cape San Blas to see what might come next. After another hearty, homemade supper of fried, fresh flounder and garden vegetables, and after putting the kids to bed, Sally returned from the upstairs with a neatly folded quilt that she handed to the doctor. "In case we want to sit on the beach," she said. "Let's take a walk. It's such a nice night. The children know to call the Winns if they have any trouble, and we won't go far."

They walked down the same path that they had traversed a few weeks before when they had first met, but now it was dark and so far from the lights of town that it seemed like they were under a vast ceiling of bright stars that lit their way on this moonless night. When they had reached the beach and removed their shoes, they held hands like teenagers and strolled silently along the smooth sand. Mercifully, there was a brisk, warm breeze coming in from the sea, just strong enough to keep the mosquitoes at bay. The beach curved after about a quarter of a mile, and she led him up into the dunes where, when they were sitting side by side, they were hidden from the ever-present beam of the lighthouse. The doctor spread the blanket, and they sat together for a while watching the sea. "So peaceful," she said. "Do you miss being married?"

"Yes, sometimes, but I'm used to being alone by now. How about you?"

"I have to admit that I don't miss Earl, but I do get lonely sometimes."

"I know the feeling," the doctor said, as he leaned back and peered into the stars. "I've gotten so used to being alone that it almost seems natural now. To be honest, not until I met you did I realize how lonely I had become. With you, I see what I've been missing. It's sad, I guess, living our lives without . . . well, not to get too sappy here . . . but without love."

"Well," she said, grasping his hand, "I've never been one to just accept something. If I was, I'd still be back in that god-awful little shack in West Texas sucking up dust. When both my mama and daddy got sick, I learned fast that I'd have to make my own way. And when Earl no longer could or would take care of us, it made me even surer that I was the only one responsible for my own happiness—no one else. So I guess I've learned by now to take what I need. And, you know what, Dr. Berber? What I need right now is you."

With that, she leaned over and kissed him passionately, as in his dream. But what followed was much better than his dream. Sally took over and led him patiently through the long-neglected preamble of love-making, until instincts took over, and they were both overcome by the pent-up feelings they had been tacitly harboring for the past few weeks.

The doctor had not been sure how he would react if, and when, this moment arrived. It had been a long time. Not only was he out of practice, but he was also past his prime, by more than a few years now. And he had, in fact, advised enough men far younger than he that they could no longer expect to perform as they once had. But, to his pleasant surprise, and owing to Sally's gentle succor, he had, he thought, performed rather adequately, if not admirably—well enough anyway that they now lay unclothed in each other's arms, breathing in unison. For once, in a long time, the doctor felt no pain, only solace and comfort, and even some semblance of serenity, next to her in the stillness of the night.

He was drifting off to sleep when Sally nudged him awake and told him it was time to start back to her house. They dressed slowly, the doctor peeking at her slight, pale figure in the glimmering starlight.

They returned along the beach, again hand in hand, their path lit by the glistening sky. As the lighthouse cottages came into view, they saw a shooting star blaze brilliantly above the horizon before evaporating into the heavens.

Standing in the shadows of her front porch light, Sally's eyes seemed suddenly sad, the doctor thought.

"What?" he asked.

She looked down and then into his eyes. "I have something to tell you," she said.

"What? What is it?"

He thought he saw her eyes beginning to tear now, but before he could comfort her, they heard a cry from inside the house.

"Mama?" a child's voice implored.

"Yes, Roseanne, it's okay," Sally answered. "What's wrong, honey?"

"I had another bad dream," Roseanne whimpered from the other side of the screen door.

"I better go in now," Sally whispered to the doctor.

"Can I help?"

"No, go home. She'll be okay. We'll talk later. Goodnight."

They kissed briefly, and the doctor, disconcerted, watched as she disappeared into the darkness of a scared child's nightmare.

Chapter Thirty-four

The doctor was slow to rise the next morning. He was glad it was Saturday because he could lie there in bed a little longer and enjoy the memory of his time with Sally Martin the night before. He wondered what she was about to tell him before they were interrupted by Roseanne's crying. At any rate, there was no doubt now that he was somehow falling in love with her, but he was still unsure about exactly where that would lead. At least, he thought, he was enjoying the trip.

After the doctor finished breakfast, he took *Their Eyes Were Watching God* out on the back porch. Even though Janie's plight in the story was so far disheartening, the doctor did enjoy the morning and the aroma of the fragrant honeysuckle flowers that were now in full bloom. Someone had left a burlap bag next to the door, and the doctor opened it to see what was inside. At first, he thought it was some sort of melon, until he got a whiff of its sour, vaguely familiar spicy odor. As he bent over to get a closer look, he found, to his horror, a disembodied, bloody ball of a human head that appeared to have been severed rather cleanly right below its stubbled chin. After dropping the bag and backing away in revulsion, the doctor forced himself to look again into the bag at the gory neck with its entrails obscenely exposed and clotted with ugly clumps of brown blood, and, as he carefully rotated the thing, at the face, eyes closed and blood-covered, but unmistakably that of Sheriff Byrd "Dog" Batson.

He looked around his backyard, down the alley, over to Miss Shriver's house next door. No one was in sight; nothing seemed amiss. He stood there on his back porch, stupefied, without the slightest idea of why the sheriff's head had been delivered to him or what, now that it had been, to do with it. All he could think of, for some unfathomable reason, was that he was glad that Jewel had not been working today and found it. She would have really been crazed. Afraid that she or someone else might inexplicably show up, he quickly took the bag and its gory contents to his car, where he placed it on the floorboard in front of the driver's side backseat.

Now what to do? Should he call Chief Lane or Judge Denton and report the receipt of his grisly gift? What to do with it? But why was it here in the first place? And who was responsible for its extraction from the rest of the sheriff? He sat there on his back porch trying to figure it all out, for how long, he wasn't sure. But at some point, the phone rang and the doctor had the answer to at least one of his questions.

"Hello, Doctor," the caller said. "This is Norm Blanchard. I'm the weekend watchman at the St. Joe Paper Company. I was just now doing my rounds and you won't believe what I found."

The doctor had a good idea that he already knew. "What?" he asked anyway.

"A bloody body. Without a head. Next to a big power saw out back."

"Any identification on him?" the doctor asked.

"Yeah, man's got on a bloody gray sheriff's uniform with a badge and all, and he's got a wallet in his back pocket with a driver's license and thirty bucks still in it. The license says he's Byrd E. Batson."

"Have you notified the police?"

"Yeah, they're on their way. I just thought maybe I should call you too."

"Well, Mr. Blanchard, I appreciate you thinking of me, but it sounds like there's nothing I can do for the sheriff now. So y'all wait for the police to show up and tell them if they need me to give me a call, okay?"

The doctor never did hear from the police, but he kept thinking all weekend about the sheriff's head and body and what must have happened and what he should do about it. By Sunday evening, when people were supposed to start arriving for Gabriel's going-away gathering, the doctor was just as confused and confounded as he was the day before when he first opened the burlap bag on his back porch.

Jewel, Marcus, and Gabriel all came in together, each carrying brown paper bags full of food for supper.

"Happy Mother's Day," the doctor said.

"Thanks, Doc," Jewel said, emptying the bags onto the kitchen counter. She seemed a little gloomy again today, the doctor thought, no doubt because of Gabriel's impending departure. "It's been a good one so far. Gabriel and Marcus took me and mama out to the Black Cat Café for dinner, but we're still gonna give Gabriel a last supper that'll make him wanna come back again and again. Let's see here. We gonna make Gabriel's favorite meal. We got some fresh okra I just picked outta mama's garden. And some lard to fry it in once I slice it up and dip it in this buttermilk and this stone-ground cornmeal. And I got a ham hock in the ice box to cook up with these black-eyed susans needin' to be shelled, so y'all git out there on the back porch and git busy, while I stir up some cornbread to go with it."

"Where's Gator?" the doctor asked.

"Ain't seen him yet," Jewel said. "But I talked to him a couple of days ago and he said he's comin'."

"Y'all hear about the sheriff?" Gabriel asked.

"Yes," the doctor said. "Isn't that something?"

"Well, after supper, when little ears ain't around," Jewel said, "I'll tell you something else about the sheriff. But now let's git busy on this here supper."

"Y'all talkin' 'bout me?" Marcus said, grabbing the bag of black-eyed peas and heading for the back porch.

Just then they heard Gator's truck skid to a long stop in the shell driveway out back. Gator, as usual, came bearing gifts. This time a gallon jug of Dr. Price's cane whiskey and a peck basket filled with freshly harvested bay scallops that Gator had just now finished dredging from the shallow seagrass beds in Indian Lagoon near his camp.

"How's my favorite mother?" Gator asked as he gathered Jewel in.

"Tryin' to slice this here okra," she said. "So be careful where you puttin' your hands if you don't want 'em cut off. Just start shuckin' them scallops. I'll fry 'em in some butter and lemon juice. Marcus, run next door and ask Miss Shriver for a handful of parsley outta her garden, so I can sprinkle that on top."

While the cornbread and black-eyed peas were cooking and Marcus was setting the table, Jewel joined the men on the back porch to have a glass of moonshine. "All right," she said, wiping her hands on her apron. "Who do you think done the sheriff in?"

"I'd guess them moonshiners," Gabriel said. "They're awful vengeful. Maybe they think the sheriff knew too much or maybe he got greedy and asked for more protection money from them."

"Well, from where the body was found," the doctor suggested, "I'd guess the St. Joe Paper Company. The sheriff told me he hated the DuPonts for running his father off his farm, and he was always over there looking around, trying to figure out what chemicals they were dumping in the bay. I think he had it in for them, and they just decided to get rid of him. These are very powerful people who own that mill, and I don't think they tolerate much meddling, especially from a backwoods sheriff."

"Could be," Gator said. "Seems like the sheriff had a lot of enemies. And the worse one's body ain't even been found yet, not to mention the sheriff's head."

"Well, I got my theory," Jewel said, "but it'll have to wait until after supper which should be about ready now. Let's go."

Gator refilled the glasses as Jewel put the bowls of black-eyed peas and fried okra and the platter of cornbread on the table. As the men passed the food around, Jewel tossed the little bay scallops briefly in a hot frying pan coated with butter and lemon juice and then finished them with a sprinkle of chopped parsley.

"To Gabriel," the doctor said, raising his glass, "may he become the next Rudy Vallee and come back in a big, red Cadillac. Although, after a meal like this, if he steals Jewel away from me, I'm liable to shoot him."

After the toast, Gator said he had an announcement to make. "I'm goin' to work for Dr. Price out on St. Vincent Island," he said. "He's phasing out the moonshining business. Says it's too much hassle. People can go about anyplace and get a drink now, so the younger generation ain't taking to his brand of whiskey anymore. Says the death of the Martin man was the last straw. So he's goin' into the oyster business. Everyone around here knows that the oysters in Big Bayou are the best in the world, so he's gonna harvest and sell them. And I'm gonna help him. Train all his moonshinin' employees how to rake them and such. I ain't givin' up my camp or nothin' drastic like that, but maybe I won't have to work so hard just to put food on the table. I'll have a regular check comin' in just like a white man. I ain't gettin' any younger, you know."

"Wow, that's great news," the doctor said, again raising his glass. "To the new Gator, may his new career prove profitable and not so time-consuming that we don't get to go hunting and fishing together now and again."

"You can bet on that, partner," Gator said.

After supper, Gabriel played his guitar and sang, and then Jewel served everyone a slice of watermelon. When they had finished and Gator broke out the Partagas cigars, Jewel put Marcus to bed in the spare bedroom upstairs.

"I gonna tell you, now that Marcus is in bed," Jewel said, sitting down next to Gabriel, "who killed the sheriff. I seen Regina Robbins this morning at church. She can be duller than a bag of hammers sometimes, but she's honest as the day is long. Well, anyway, she's the night clerk out at Wimico Lake Cabins. She tells me, now that the sheriff is dead, she can tell me who's been beatin' up all them colored prostitutes. It's the sheriff, she said. Says that he brings them girls out there to the cabins, rents a room for the night, and then sometime before morning them girls come out all beat up. He told Regina that if she say a word, she'd end up like them. So you know some colored men they work out at that mill and I betcha more than one of 'em knows how to work a power saw. So my guess is one of them whores had had enough and seen that his head got sawed off."

"Makes sense to me," the doctor said. He had to agree with Gator; the man did seem to have a lot of enemies.

Later, after Gator had passed out on the living room couch and Gabriel was carrying the sleeping Marcus to the car, Jewel ushered the doctor into the kitchen and told him what else Regina Robbins had told her at church that morning.

Chapter Thirty-five

After Jewel and Marcus and Gabriel had gone home, the doctor got in his car and drove to the Cape San Blas Lighthouse. The night was so unseasonably cool that he turned the car's heater on to keep warm. The full moon was bright enough that he could have driven the familiar road to the cape without his lights on, but he didn't. But as he drove he had to wonder, after what Jewel had told him, if the old curse that had bedeviled the town for so many years was still alive. Maybe, despite the new mill and the sheriff's death, it was just too implacable to go away.

It was getting close to midnight, so he was surprised to find Harvey Winn in a blue, wool jacket huddled in his rocking chair, out on his front porch, smoking his pipe, as usual, and staring out to sea. Did the man never sleep? So the doctor stopped to say hello to the lighthouse keeper, but this time he asked if he could join him for a minute. Sitting next to each other on the porch, Harvey told him that he had started his new job at the paper mill, but that he had not found a place to live in town yet. Mary, his wife, continued to insist that it be far away from Sally Martin, but Harvey was so far unable to locate anything suitable.

Since the lighthouse service had still not hired a replacement for him, he was maintaining the light the best he could in exchange for his family's continued use of the keeper's cottage. The doctor asked him if he had worked at the mill on Friday night when the sheriff had been killed. Harvey said that he had been at work that night, but he hadn't noticed anything unusual.

"It's a big place, Doc," he said. "It takes me pretty near a shift to get around the whole plant. And that night I didn't see a thing. I can see plenty, though, just sitting right here on my front porch."

"Like what?" the doctor inquired.

As Harvey told the doctor some of the things he had observed and the two continued to talk there on the keeper's front porch, the doctor noticed a light coming on in Sally Martin's kitchen. So, after a while, the doctor said goodnight to the lighthouse keeper and walked over to Sally's cottage. He knocked on the back door and Sally, looking a little weary, let him in.

"Having a cup of tea," she said. "Care to join me? What brings you out here at this hour of the night?"

"No, no thank you. But I wouldn't mind a glass of water, if you don't mind. I couldn't sleep, so I decided to take a drive. I was hoping you might still be up."

As she filled a glass with water from the kitchen sink, the doctor stared. She looked particularly appealing, he thought, in her blue chenille bathrobe and long, curly red hair which appeared to have just been washed and brushed.

"How about you? You're up late too. I really didn't expect to find you awake," the doctor said, as he sat down with her at the kitchen table.

"I couldn't sleep either. With all that's gone on in the past few weeks, my head's spinning."

"You heard about the sheriff then?"

"Yes, how tragic. Do they have any idea what happened?" she asked.

"No, I don't think so. I thought maybe you did."

"Me?" she said. "What on earth are you talking about?"

"Look, Sally, I think it's time you leveled with me. I know about you and Sheriff Batson. I know you and him have been meeting secretly at the Wimico Lake Cabins for more than half a year now. That you've been leaving your kids asleep while Earl is out carousing, and that you've been walking up the road to meet the sheriff and then driving over to the Cabins to do the things that people do out there."

"How do you know that?" she asked in astonishment.

"Let's put it this way, Sally, this is a small town. Nothing is kept secret very long here. My maid Jewel doesn't know how to get me to clear the table, but she knows about everything else that goes on around here, and your neighbor Harvey Winn, who's in love with you, by the way, seems harmless enough, but he sees more than you might realize from his rocker on the front porch over there. When did you and the sheriff decide to kill your husband?"

She looked into her cup of tea for a very long time before speaking, as if the right answer might somehow lie within it. The doctor waited silently; he was in no hurry to hear the truth. In fact, in some way, he wished that she would lie to him again, so that he could be surer of the noxious mixture of anger and sadness that was welling up inside of him.

"Just after the first of the year," she finally said, the tears filling her eyes. "After Earl refused to give me a divorce. I upped the value of the insurance policy without him knowing about it. I forged his signature and paid the premiums. He didn't even notice."

"Then you and the sheriff hired someone to kill him?"

"Yes," she said, the tears now streaming down her cheeks. "That is, Byrd arranged it with this lunatic Lucky and unfortunately I went along with it."

"If the sheriff hired Lucky, then why did he kill him?"

"Well," she said between sobs, "Lucky got greedy. We had agreed on a price, but he decided he wanted more and stuck around here and then wrote that stupid note to me. I was prepared to pay him just to get rid of him, and I thought you could help me do that, since, by this time, I was afraid for myself and the kids. But you had to bring the sheriff in, and the sheriff decided that Lucky's usefulness was at an end. And, if it hadn't been for your friend Reggie, it all would have been over. Lucky would have disappeared forever and no one would be the wiser."

"Except Gator and me, as it turned out, until the sheriff convinced us that it was best to let sleeping dogs lie and forget about the whole thing. Which we did, sort of—that is, until the sheriff turned up dead too."

The doctor watched her cry for a while. His urge was to go to her and comfort her, as usual, but first he wanted to get to the end of this story no matter where it led.

"You know, don't you," the doctor said, "that the sheriff was not a very good man?"

"At first I thought he was. He was very kind to me, from the first night I met him when I went to get Earl out of the drunk tank in Wewa and Byrd let him go for free because I didn't have the cash. Then he helped me buy the kids food and clothes when Earl had gambled everything away. At first, he was very generous and kind. And like Earl, I thought I could make him happy."

"Did you?"

"No, not really. Like Earl, he harbored so much unhappiness that it was finally impossible to rid him of it."

"So you found out he was not so nice after all?"

"Yes," she said between sobs. "He turned out to be not so nice, mean sometimes, and rough, if you know what I mean. But by then it was too late. Earl was gone. And I didn't know what to do. Then you came along.

Unreasonably, I fell for you. I needed you. And you were always there for me—unselfishly. Not like Earl . . . or Byrd. In the end, Byrd had to go."

"To go?" the doctor asked, unsure of what she was telling him. "Like Earl?"

The house was quiet as the doctor leaned forward to hear her answer. She looked up from her tea, wiped away her tears with the sleeve of her robe, and for the first time that evening looked straight into the doctor's eyes.

"Why would I want to share the insurance money with a man like that?" she whispered.

* * *

The Indian Pass Raw Bar was still lit when the doctor drove past it, but only three cars were parked in front of it. When he reached the narrow channel called Indian Pass that joined Apalachicola Bay to the Gulf of Mexico at St. Vincent Island, he parked the car on the side of the road and waited for a few minutes to make sure he was alone. All he heard was a chorus of noisy cicadas and the water gently lapping at the shore, a dog barking somewhere in the distance.

He got out of the car and walked to the ocean's edge. Despite its placid appearance, the current was strong and steady here at the pass, powerful enough to take a man's body out to sea in a matter of minutes. All he had to do was jump in and he'd be gone for good. Maybe not entirely painless, he thought, but relatively quick and certain.

He stared into the swift water for a long time and then returned to his car and pulled the burlap bag from the floor of the backseat and carried it to the edge of the channel. It was heavier than he remembered. The moon was full and the sky was alight in a symphony of stars. With the phosphorescence of the sea, his path was as light as daybreak. Hopefully, there was no one nearby to see him, because he was readily visible standing there, shivering on the white sandy seashore. Oh well, no matter now. He stared at the moon for a moment, then reared back on his heels and flung the sack as far up and out into the channel as he could see, where he knew the rapid current would soon carry it far away into the bay.

As he returned to his old Ford, the doctor could not be sure, with his failing eyesight, but he thought he saw, just out of the corner of his right eye, a curly-haired figure, awash in the moon glow, silently disappearing into the shadows of the shimmering pines.

Here are some other books from Pineapple Press on related topics. For a complete catalog, visit our website at www.pineapplepress.com. Or write to Pineapple Press, P.O. Box 3889, Sarasota, Florida 34230-3889, or call (800) 746-3275.

Conflict of Interest by Terry Lewis. Trial lawyer Ted Stevens fights his own battles, including his alcoholism and his pending divorce, as he fights for his client in a murder case. But it's the other suspect in the case who causes the conflict of interest. Ted must choose between concealing evidence that would be helpful to his client or revealing it, thereby becoming a suspect himself. (hb)

Death in Bloodhound Red by Virginia Lanier. Jo Beth Sidden raises and trains bloodhounds for search-and-rescue missions in the Okefenokee Swamp. She is used to dealing with lost kids, prison escapees, snakes, bugs, macho deputies, and her abusive ex-husband. But now she is suspected of murder and has to choose between betraying a friend and proving her innocence. (pb)

Mystery in the Sunshine State, edited by Stuart Kaminsky. Offers a selection of Florida mysteries from many of Florida's notable writers. Follow professional investigators and amateur sleuths alike as they patiently uncover clues to finally reveal the identity of a killer or the answer to a riddle. (pb)

Seven Mile Bridge by Michael Biehl. A Florida Keys dive shop owner with a taste for whiskey and not much else returns home to Wisconsin after his mother's death, searching for clues to his father's death years before. He is stunned by what he learns about his father's life. Mostly, he is surprised by what he learns about himself. Fluidly moving between past and present, hope and despair, *Seven Mile Bridge* is a story about one man's obsession with the truth and how much can depend on finding it. (hb)

CPSIA information can be obtained at www.ICGtesting.com
Printed in the USA
BVOW011030020212

281890BV00001B/1/P

9 781561 645145